BEN,
THE LUGGAGE BOY

BEN,
THE LUGGAGE BOY

OR

AMONG THE WHARVES

By

HORATIO ALGER, JR.,

AUTHOR OF
"RAGGED DICK," "FAME AND FORTUNE,"
"MARK, THE MATCH BOY," "ROUGH AND READY,"
"CAMPAIGN SERIES," "LUCK AND PLUCK SERIES,"
ETC.

BottomoftheHillPublishing.com

ISBN: 978-1-4837-0545-3

TO
ANNIE,
THIS VOLUME IS DEDICATED
In Tender Remembrance
BY HER
AFFECTIONATE BROTHER

PREFACE

In presenting "Ben, the Luggage Boy," to the public, as the fifth of the Ragged Dick Series, the author desires to say that it is in all essential points a true history; the particulars of the story having been communicated to him, by Ben himself, nearly two years since. In particular, the circumstances attending the boy's running away from home, and adopting the life of a street boy, are in strict accordance with Ben's own statement. While some of the street incidents are borrowed from the writer's own observation, those who are really familiar with the different phases which street life assumes in New York, will readily recognize their fidelity. The chapter entitled "The Room under the Wharf" will recall to many readers of the daily journals a paragraph which made its appearance within two years. The writer cannot close without expressing anew his thanks for the large share of favor which has been accorded to the volumes of the present series, and takes this opportunity of saying that, in their preparation, invention has played but a subordinate part. For his delineations of character and choice of incidents, he has been mainly indebted to his own observation, aided by valuable communications and suggestions from those who have been brought into familiar acquaintance with the class whose mode of life he has sought to describe.

New York, April 5, 1876.

Content

CHAPTER I

INTRODUCES BEN, THE LUGGAGE BOY

"How much yer made this mornin', Ben?"

"Nary red," answered Ben, composedly.

"Had yer breakfast?"

"Only an apple. That's all I've eaten since yesterday. It's most time for the train to be in from Philadelphy. I'm layin' round for a job."

The first speaker was a short, freckled-faced boy, whose box strapped to his back identified him at once as a street boot-black. His hair was red, his fingers defaced by stains of blacking, and his clothing constructed on the most approved system of ventilation. He appeared to be about twelve years old.

The boy whom he addressed as Ben was taller, and looked older. He was probably not far from sixteen. His face and hands, though browned by exposure to wind and weather, were several shades cleaner than those of his companion. His face, too, was of a less common type. It was easy to see that, if he had been well dressed, he might readily have been taken for a gentleman's son. But in his present attire there was little chance of this mistake being made. His pants, marked by a green stripe, small around the waist and very broad at the hips, had evidently once belonged to a Bowery swell; for the Bowery has its swells as well as Broadway, its more aristocratic neighbor. The vest had been discarded as a needless luxury, its place being partially supplied by a shirt of thick red flannel. This was covered by a frock-coat, which might once have belonged to a member of the Fat Men's Association, being alder-manic in its proportions. Now it was fallen from its high estate, its nap and original gloss had long departed, and it was frayed and torn in many places. But among the street-boys dress is not much regarded, and Ben never thought of apologizing for the defects of his wardrobe. We shall learn in time what were his faults and what his virtues, for I can assure my readers that street boys do have virtues sometimes, and when they are thoroughly convinced that a questioner feels an interest in them will drop the "chaff" in which they commonly indulge, and talk seriously and feelingly of their faults and hardships. Some do this for a purpose, no doubt, and the verdant stranger is liable to be taken in by assumed virtue, and waste sympathy on those who do not deserve it. But there are also many boys who have good tendencies and aspirations, and only need to be encouraged and placed under right influences to develop into worthy and respectable men.

The conversation recorded above took place at the foot of Cortlandt Street, opposite the ferry wharf. It was nearly time for the train, and there was the usual scene of confusion. Express wagons, hacks, boys, laborers, were gathering, presenting a confusing medley to the eye of one unaccustomed to the spectacle.

Ben was a luggage boy, his occupation being to wait at the piers for the arrival of steamboats, or at the railway stations, on the chance of getting a carpet-bag or valise to carry. His business was a precarious one. Sometimes he was lucky, sometimes unlucky. When he was flush, he treated himself to a "square meal," and finished up the day at Tony Pastor's, or the Old Bowery, where from his seat in the pit he indulged in independent criticism of the acting, as he leaned back in his seat and munched peanuts, throwing the shells about carelessly.

It is not surprising that the street-boys like the Old Bowery, and are willing to stint their stomachs, or run the risk of a night in the streets, for the sake of the warm room and the glittering illusions of the stage, introducing them for the time being to the society of nobles and ladies of high birth, and enabling them to forget for a time the hardships of their own lot, while they follow with rapt interest the fortunes of Lord Frederic Montressor or the Lady Imogene Delacour. Strange as it may seem, the street Arab has a decided fancy for these pictures of aristocracy, and never suspects their want of fidelity. When the play ends, and Lord Frederic comes to his own, having foiled all the schemes of his crafty and unprincipled enemies, no one rejoices more than the ragged boy who has sat through the evening an interested spectator of the play, and in his pleasure at the successful denouement, he almost forgets that he will probably find the Newsboys' Lodging House closed for the night, and be compelled to take up with such sleeping accommodations as the street may provide.

Ben crossed the street, taking a straight course, without paying especial attention to the mud, which caused other pedestrians to pick their way. To the condition of his shoes he was supremely indifferent. Stockings he did not wear. They are luxuries in which few street boys indulge.

He had not long to wait. The boat bumped against the wharf, and directly a crowd of passengers poured through the open gates in a continuous stream.

Ben looked sharply around him to judge who would be likely to employ him. His attention was drawn to an elderly lady, with a large carpet-bag swelled almost to bursting. She was looking about her in a bewildered manner.

"Carry your bag, ma'am?" he said, at the same time motioning towards it.

"Who be you?" asked the old lady, suspiciously.

"I'm a baggage-smasher," said Ben.

"Then I don't want you," answered the old lady, clinging to her bag as if she feared it would be wrested from her. "I'm surprised that the law allows sich things. You might be in a better business, young man, than smashing baggage."

"That's where you're right, old lady," said Ben.

"Bankin' would pay better, if I only had the money to start on."

"Are you much acquainted in New York?" asked the old lady.

"Yes," said Ben; "I know the mayor 'n' aldermen, 'n' all the principal men. A. T. Stooart's my intimate friend, and I dine with Vanderbilt every Sunday when I aint engaged at Astor's."

"Do you wear them clo'es when you visit your fine friends?" asked the old lady, shrewdly.

"No," said Ben. "Them are my every-day clo'es. I've got some velvet clo'es to home, embroidered with gold."

"I believe you are telling fibs," said the old lady. "What I want to know is, if you know my darter, Mrs. John Jones; her first name is Seraphiny. She lives on Bleecker Street, and her husband, who is a nice man, though his head is bald on top, keeps a grocery store."

"Of course I do," said Ben. "It was only yesterday that she told me her mother was comin' to see her. I might have knowed you was she."

"How would you have knowed?"

"Cause she told me just how you looked."

"Did she? How did she say I looked?"

"She said you was most ninety, and—"

"It isn't true," said the old lady, indignantly. "I'm only seventy-three, and everybody says I'm wonderful young-lookin' for my years. I don't believe Seraphiny told you so."

"She might have said you looked as if you was most ninety."

"You're a sassy boy!" said the owner of the carpet-bag, indignantly. "I don't see how I'm going to get up to Seraphiny's," she continued, complainingly. "They'd ought to have come down to meet me. How much will you charge to carry my carpet-bag, and show me the way to my darter's?"

"Fifty cents," said Ben.

"Fifty cents!" repeated the old lady, aghast. "I didn't think you'd charge more'n ten."

"I have to," said Ben. "Board's high in New York."

"How much would they charge me in a carriage? Here you, sir," addressing a hackman, "what'll you charge to carry me to my darter's house, Mrs. John Jones, in Bleecker Street?"

"What's the number?"

"I think it's a hundred and sixty-three."

"A dollar and a half."

"A dollar 'n' a half? Couldn't you do it for less?"

"Carry your bag, sir?" asked Ben, of a gentleman passing.

The gentleman shook his head.

He made one or two other proposals, which being in like manner unsuccessful, he returned to the old lady, who, having by this time got through her negotiations with the hackman, whom she had vainly striven to beat down to seventy-five cents, was in a more favorable mood to accept Ben's services.

"Can't you take less than fifty cents?" she asked.

"No," said Ben, decidedly.

"I'll give you forty."

"Couldn't do it," said Ben, who felt sure of gaining his point now.

"Well, I suppose I shall be obleeged to hire you," said the old lady with a sigh. "Seraphiny ought to have sent down to meet me. I didn't tell her I was comin' to-day; but she might have thought I'd come, bein' so pleasant. Here, you boy, you may take the bag, and mind you don't run away with it. There aint nothin' in it but some of my clo'es."

"I don't want none of your clo'es," said Ben. "My wife's bigger'n you, and they wouldn't fit her."

"Massy sakes! you aint married, be you?"

"Why shouldn't I be?"

"I don't believe it. You're not old enough. But I'm glad you don't want the clo'es. They wouldn't be of no use to you. Just you take the bag, and I'll foller on behind."

"I want my pay first."

"I aint got the change. My darter Seraphiny will pay you when we get to her house."

"That don't go down," said Ben, decidedly. "Payment in advance; that's the way I do business."

"You'll get your pay; don't you be afraid."

"I know I shall; but I want it now."

"You won't run away after I've paid you, will you?"

"In course not. That aint my style."

The old lady took out her purse, and drew therefrom forty-seven cents. She protested that she had not a cent more. Ben pardoned the deficiency, feeling that he would, notwithstanding, be well paid for his time.

"All right," said he, magnanimously. "I don't mind the three cents. It aint any object to a man of my income. Take my hand, old lady, and we'll go across the street."

"I'm afraid of bein' run over," said she, hesitatingly.

"What's the odds if you be?" said Ben. "The city'll have to pay you damages."

"But if I got killed, that wouldn't do me any good," remarked the old lady, sensibly.

"Then the money'd go to your friends," said Ben, consolingly.

"Do you think I will be run over?" asked the old lady, anxiously.

"In course you won't. I'll take care of you. They wouldn't dare to run over me," said Ben, confidently.

Somewhat reassured by this remark, the old lady submitted to Ben's guidance, and was piloted across the street in safety.

"I wouldn't live in New York for a heap of money. It would be as much as my life is worth," she remarked. "How far is Bleecker Street?"

"About two miles."

"I almost wish I'd rid. But a dollar and a half is a sight to pay."

"You'd have to pay more than that."

"That's all the man asked."

"I know," said Ben; "but when he'd got you there, he'd have charged you five dollars."

"I wouldn't have paid it."

"Yes, you would," said Ben.

"He couldn't make me."

"If you didn't pay, he'd have locked you in, and driven you off to the river, and dumped you in."

"Do they ever do such things?" asked the old lady, startled.

"In course they do. Only last week a beautiful young lady was served that way, 'cause she wouldn't pay what the hackman wanted."

"And what was done to him?"

"Nothin'," said Ben. "The police is in league with 'em, and get their share of the money."

"Why, you don't say so! What a wicked place New York is, to be sure!"

"Of course it is. It's so wicked I'm goin' to the country myself as soon as I get money enough to buy a farm."

"Have you got much money saved up?" asked the old lady, interested.

"Four thousand six hundred and seventy-seven dollars and fifty-five cents. I don't count this money you give me, 'cause I'm goin' to spend it."

"You didn't make it all carryin' carpet-bags," said the old lady, incredulously.

"No, I made most of it spekilatin' in real estate," said Ben.

"You don't say!"

"Yes, I do."

"You've got most enough to buy a farm a'ready."

"I aint goin' to buy till I can buy a good one."

"What's the name of this street?"

"West Broadway."

They were really upon West Broadway by this time, that being as direct a line as any to Bleecker Street.

"You see that store," said Ben.

"Yes; what's the matter of it?"

"I don't own it *now*," said Ben. "I sold it, cos the tenants didn't pay their rent reg'lar."

"I should think you'd dress better if you've got so much money," said the old lady, not unnaturally.

"What's the use of wearin' nice clo'es round among the wharves?" said Ben.

"There's suthin in that. I tell my darter Jane—she lives in the country—that it's no use dressin' up the children to go to school,—they're sure to get their clo'es tore and dirty afore they get home."

So Ben beguiled the way with wonderful stories, with which he played upon the old lady's credulity. Of course it was wrong; but a street education is not very likely to inspire its pupils with a reverence for truth; and Ben had been knocking about the streets of New York, most of the time among the wharves, for six years. His street education had commenced at the age of ten. He had adopted it of his own free will. Even now there was a comfortable home waiting for him; there were parents who supposed him dead, and who would have found a difficulty in recognizing him under his present circumstances. In the next chapter a light will be thrown upon his past history, and the reader will learn how his street life began.

CHAPTER II

HOW BEN COMMENCED HIS STREET LIFE

One pleasant morning, six years before the date at which this story commences, a small coasting-vessel drew up at a North River pier in the lower part of the city. It was loaded with freight, but there was at least one passenger on board. A boy of ten, dressed in a neat jacket and pants of gray-mixed cloth, stood on deck, watching with interest the busy city which they had just reached.

"Well, bub, here we are," said the captain as he passed. "I suppose you know your way home."

"Yes, sir."

"Are you going on shore now?"

"Yes, sir."

"Well, good luck to you, my lad. If you are ever down this way, when I'm in port, I shall be glad to see you."

"Thank you, sir; good-by."

"Good-by."

Ben clambered over the side, and stepped upon the wharf. In the great city he knew no one, and he was an utter stranger to the streets, never before having visited it. He was about to begin life for himself at the age of ten. He had voluntarily undertaken to support himself, leaving behind him a comfortable home, where he had been well cared for. I must explain how this came about.

Ben had a pleasant face, and would be considered good-looking. But there was a flash in his eye, when aroused, which showed that he had a quick temper, and there was an expression of firmness, unusual to one so young, which might have been read by an experienced physiognomist. He was quick-tempered, proud, and probably obstinate. Yet with these qualities he was pleasant in his manners, and had a sense of humor, which made him a favorite among his companions.

His father was a coal-dealer in a town a few miles distant from Philadelphia, of a hasty temper like Ben himself. A week before he had punished Ben severely for a fault which he had not committed. The boy's pride revolted at the injustice, and, young as he was, he resolved to run away. I suppose there are few boys who do not form this resolution at some time or other in their lives; but as a general thing it amounts to nothing. With Ben it was different. His was a strong nature, whether for good or for evil, and when he decided to do anything he was not easily moved from his resolve. He forgot, in the present case, that, though he had been unjustly punished, the injustice was not intentional on the part of his father, who had been under a wrong impression respecting him. But right or wrong, Ben made up his mind to run away; and he did so. It was two or three days before a good opportunity presented itself. Then, with a couple of shirts and collars rolled up in a small bundle, he made his escape to Philadelphia, and after roaming about the streets for several hours he made his way to the wharves, where he found a vessel bound for New York. Representing to the captain that he lived in New York, and had no money to pay his passage home, that officer, who was a good-natured man, agreed to carry him for nothing.

The voyage was now over, and Ben landed, as we have said, an utter stranger, with very indefinite ideas as to how he was to make his living. He had told the captain that he knew his way home, for having falsely represented that he lived in New York, he was in a manner compelled to this additional falsehood. Still, in spite of his friendless condition, his spirits were very good. The sun shone brightly; all looked animated and cheerful. Ben saw numbers of men at work about him, and he thought, "It will be a pity if I cannot make a living."

He did not care to linger about the wharf, for the captain might be led to doubt his story. Accordingly he crossed the street, and at a venture turned up a street facing the wharf.

Ben did not know much about New York, even by report. But he had heard of Broadway,—as who has not?—and this was about all he did know. When, therefore, he had gone a short distance, he ventured to ask a boot-black, whom he encountered at the corner of the next block, "Can you tell me the shortest way to Broadway?"

"Follow your nose, Johnny," was the reply.

"My name isn't Johnny," replied Ben, rather indignant at the familiarity. He had not learned that, in New York, Johnny is the generic name for boy, where the specific name is unknown.

"Aint it though?" returned the boot-black "What's the price of turnips out where you live?"

"I'll make your nose turn up if you aint careful," retorted Ben, wrathfully.

"You'll do," said the boot-black, favorably impressed by Ben's pluck. "Just go straight ahead, and you'll come to Broadway. I'm going that way, and you can come along with me if you want to."

"Thank you," said Ben, appeased by the boy's changed manner.

"Are you going to stay here?" inquired his new acquaintance.

"Yes," said Ben; "I'm going to live here."

"Where do your friends live?"

"I haven't got any friends in New York," said Ben, with a little hesitation.

"Over in Brooklyn, or Jersey, maybe?"

"No, I don't know anybody this way."

"Whew!" whistled the other. "How you goin' to live?"

"I expect to earn my living," said Ben, in a tone of importance.

"Father and mother dead?"

"No, they're alive."

"I s'pose they're poor?"

"No, they're not; they're well off."

The boot-black looked puzzled.

"Why didn't you stay at home then? Wouldn't they let you?"

"Of course they would. The fact is, I've run away."

"Maybe they'd adopt me instead of you."

"I don't think they would," said Ben, laughing.

"I wish somebody with lots of cash would adopt me, and make a gentleman of me. It would be a good sight better'n blackin' boots."

"Do you make much money that way?" inquired Ben.

"Pleasant days like this, sometimes I make a dollar, but when it rains there aint much doin'."

"How much have you made this morning?" asked Ben, with interest.

"Sixty cents."

"Sixty cents, and it isn't more than ten o'clock. That's doing pretty well."

"'Taint so good in the afternoon. Most everybody gets their boots blacked in the mornin'. What are you goin' to do?"

"I don't know," said Ben.

"Goin' to black boots? I'll show you how," said the other, generously overlooking all considerations of possible rivalry.

"I don't think I should like that very well," said Ben, slowly.

Having been brought up in a comfortable home, he had a prejudice in favor of clean hands and unsoiled clothes,—a prejudice of which his street life speedily cured him.

"I think I should rather sell papers, or go into a store," said Ben.

"You can't make so much money sellin' papers," said his new

acquaintance. "Then you might get 'stuck'".

"What's that?" inquired Ben, innocently.

"Don't you know?" asked the boot-black, wonderingly. "Why, it's when you've got more papers than you can sell. That's what takes off the profits. I was a newsboy once; but it's too hard work for the money. There aint no chance of gettin' stuck on my business."

"It's rather a dirty business," said Ben, venturing to state his main objection, at the risk of offending. But Jerry Collins, for that was his name, was not very sensitive on this score.

"What's the odds?" he said, indifferently. "A feller gets used to it."

Ben looked at Jerry's begrimed hands, and clothes liberally marked with spots of blacking, and he felt that he was not quite ready to get used to appearing in public in this way. He was yet young in his street life. The time came when he ceased to be so particular.

"Where do you board?" asked Ben, after a little pause.

Jerry Collins stared at the questioner as if he suspected that a joke was intended. But Ben's serious face assured him that he was in earnest.

"You're jolly green," he remarked, sententiously.

"Look here," said Ben, with spirit, "I'll give you a licking if you say that again."

It may be considered rather singular that Jerry, Instead of resenting this threat, was led by it to regard Ben with favor.

"I didn't mean anything," he said, by way of apology. "You're a trump, and you'll get over it when you've been in the city a week."

"What made you call me green?" asked Ben.

"Did you think I boarded up to the Fifth Avenue?" asked Jerry.

"What's that,—a hotel?"

"Yes, it's one of the big hotels, where they eat off gold plates."

"No, I don't suppose you board there," said Ben, laughing; "but I suppose there are cheaper boarding-places. Where do you sleep?"

"Sometimes in wagons, or in door-ways, on the docks, or anywhere where I get a chance."

"Don't you get cold sleeping out-doors?" asked Ben.

"Oh, I'm used to it," said Jerry. "When it's cold I go to the Lodging House."

"What's that?"

Jerry explained that there was a Newsboys' Lodging House, where a bed could be obtained for six cents a night.

"That's cheap," said Ben.

"'Taint so cheap as sleepin' out-doors," returned the boot-black.

This was true; but Ben thought he would rather pay the six cents than sleep out, if it were only for the damage likely to come to his clothes, which were yet clean and neat. Looking at Jerry's suit, however, he saw that this consideration would be likely to have less weight with him. He began to understand that he had entered upon a very different life from the one he had hitherto led. He was not easily daunted, however.

"If he can stand it, I can," he said to himself.

CHAPTER III

STREET SCENES

"Here's Broadway," said Jerry, suddenly.

They emerged from the side street on which they had been walking, and, turning the corner, found themselves in the great thoroughfare, a block or two above Trinity Church.

Ben surveyed the busy scenes that opened before him, with the eager interest of a country boy who saw them for the first time.

"What church is that?" he asked, pointing to the tall spire of the imposing church that faces Wall Street.

"That's Trinity Church."

"Do you go to church there?"

"I don't go anywhere else," said Jerry, equivocally. "What's the use of going to church?"

"I thought everybody went to church," said Ben, speaking from his experience in a country village "that is, most everybody," he corrected himself, as several persons occurred to his mind who were more punctual in their attendance at the liquor saloon than the church.

"If I'd got good clothes like you have I'd go once just to see what it's like; but I'd a good sight rather go to the old Bowery Theatre."

"But you ought not to say that," said Ben, a little startled.

"Why not?"

"Because it's better to go to church than to the theatre."

"Is it?" said Jerry. "Well, you can go if you want to. I'd give more for a stunnin' old play at the Bowery than fifty churches."

Ben began to suspect that Jerry was rather loose in his ideas on the subject of religion, but did not think it best to say so, for fear of giving offence, though in all probability Jerry's sensitiveness would not have been at all disturbed by such a charge.

During the last portion of the conversation they had been standing still at the street corner.

"I'm goin' to Nassau Street," said Jerry. "If you want to go up Broadway, that's the way."

Without waiting for an answer he darted across the street, threading his way among the numerous vehicles with a coolness and a success which amazed Ben, who momentarily expected to see him run over. He drew a long breath when he saw him safe on the other side, and bethought himself that he would not like to take a similar risk. He felt sorry to have Jerry leave him so abruptly. The boot-black had already imparted to him considerable information about New York, which he saw was likely to be of benefit to him. Besides, he felt that any society was better than solitude, and a sudden feeling of loneliness overpowered him, as he felt that among the crowd of persons that jostled him as he stood at the corner, there was not one who felt an interest in him, or even knew his name. It was very different in his native village, where he knew everybody, and everybody had a friendly word for him. The thought did occur to him for a moment whether he had been wise in running away from home; but the thought of the unjust punishment came with it, and his expression became firmer and more resolute.

"I won't go home if I starve," he said proudly to himself; and armed with this new resolution he proceeded up Broadway.

His attention was soon drawn to the street merchants doing business on the sidewalk. Here was a vender of neckties, displaying a varied assortment of different colors, for "only twenty-five cents each." Next came a candy merchant with his stock in trade, divided up into irregular lumps, and labelled a penny apiece. They looked rather tempting, and Ben would have purchased, but he knew very well that his cash capital amounted to only twenty-five cents, which, considering that he was as yet without an income, was likely to be wanted for other purposes.

Next came a man with an assortment of knives, all of them open, and sticking into a large board, which was the only shop required by their proprietor. Ben stopped a moment to look at them. He had always had a fancy for knives, but was now without one. In fact he had sold a handsome knife, which he had received as a birthday present, for seventy-five cents, to raise money for his present expedition. Of this sum but twenty-five cents remained.

"Will you buy a knife to-day, young gentleman?" asked the vender, who was on the alert for customers.

"No, I guess not," said Ben.

"Here's a very nice one for only one dollar," said the street merchant, taking up a showy-looking knife with three blades. "Its the best of steel, warranted. You won't get another such knife for the price in the city."

It did look cheap certainly. Ben could not but allow that. He would like to have owned it, but circumstances forbade.

"No, I won't buy to-day," he said.

"Here, you shall have it for ninety-four cents," and the vender began to roll it up in a piece of paper. "You can't say it isn't cheap."

"Yes, it's cheap enough," said Ben, moving away, "but I haven't got the money with me."

This settled the matter, and the dealer reluctantly unrolled it, and replaced it among his stock.

"If you'll call round to-morrow, I'll save it for you till then," he said.

"All right," said Ben.

"I wonder," he thought, "whether he would be so anxious to sell, if he knew that I had run away from home, and had but twenty-five cents in the world?"

Ben's neat dress deceived the man, who naturally supposed him to belong to a city family well to do.

Our young hero walked on till he came to the Astor House. He stood on the steps a few minutes taking a view of what may be considered the liveliest and most animated part of New York. Nearly opposite was Barnum's American Museum, the site being now occupied by the costly and elegant Herald Building and Park Bank. He looked across to the lower end of the City Hall Park, not yet diverted from its original purpose for the new Post Office building. He saw a procession of horse-cars in constant motion up and down Park Row. Everything seemed lively and animated; and again the thought came to Ben, "If there is employment for all these people, there must be something for me to do."

He crossed to the foot of the Park, and walked up on the Park Row side. Here again he saw a line of street merchants. Most conspicuous were the dealers in penny ballads, whose wares lined the railings, and were various enough to suit every taste. Here was an old woman, who might have gained a first prize for ugliness, presiding over an apple-stand.

"Take one, honey; it's only two cints," she said, observing that Ben's attention was drawn to a rosy-cheeked apple.

Ben was rather hungry, and reflecting that probably apples were as cheap as any other article of diet, he responded to the appeal by purchasing. It proved to be palatable, and he ate it with a good relish.

"Ice-cream, only a penny a glass," was the next announcement. The glasses, to be sure, were of very small size. Still ice-cream in any quantity for a penny seemed so ridiculously cheap that Ben, poor as he was, could not resist the temptation.

"I'll take a glass," he said.

A dab of ice-cream was deposited in a glass, and with a pewter spoon handed to Ben. He raised the spoon to his mouth, but alas! the mixture was not quite so tempting to the taste as to the eye and the pocket. It might be ice-cream, but there was an indescribable flavor about it, only to be explained on the supposition that the ice had been frozen dish-water. Ben's taste had not been educated up to that point which would enable him to relish it. He laid it down with an involuntary contortion of the face.

"Give it to me, Johnny," he heard at his elbow.

Turning, he saw a small, dirty-faced boy of six, with bare feet and tattered attire, who was gazing with a look of greedy desire at the delicious mixture.

Ben handed him the glass and spoon, and stood by, looking at him with some curiosity as he disposed of the contents with a look of evident enjoyment.

"Do you like it?" he asked.

"It's bully," said the young epicure.

If Ben had not been restricted by his narrow means, he would have purchased another glass for the urchin. It would have been a very cheap "treat." But our young adventurer reflected that he had but twenty-two cents left, and prudence forbade.

"I don't see how he can like the nasty stuff," he thought.

But the time was to come when Ben himself, grown less fastidious, would be able to relish food quite as uninviting.

Ben made his way across the Park to Broadway again. He felt that it was high time for him to be seeking employment. His ideas on this subject were not very well defined, but when he left home he made up his mind that he would try to get a place in a store on Broadway. He supposed that, among the great number of stores, there would be a chance for him to get into some one. He expected to make enough to live in a comfortable boarding-house, and buy his clothes, though he supposed that would be about all. He expected to have to economize on spending money the first year, but the second year his wages would be raised, and then it would come easier. All this shows how very verdant and unpractical our young adventurer was, and what disappointment he was preparing for himself.

However, Ben's knowledge was to come by experience, and that before long.

Reaching Broadway, he walked up slowly on the west side, looking in at the shop-windows. In the lower part of this busy street are many wholesale houses, while the upper part is devoted principally to retail shops. Coming to a large warehouse for the sale of ready-made clothing, Ben thought he might as well begin there. In such a large place there must be a good deal to do.

He passed in and looked about him rather doubtfully. The counters, which were numerous, were filled high with ready-made garments. Ben saw no one as small as himself, and that led him to doubt whether his size might not be an objection.

"Well, sonny, what do you want?" asked a clerk.

"Don't you want to hire a boy?" asked our young adventurer, plunging into his business.

"I suppose you have had considerable experience in the business?" said the clerk inclined to banter him a little.

"No, I haven't," said Ben, frankly.

"Indeed, I judged from your looks that you were a man of experience."

"If you don't want to hire me, I'll go," said Ben, independently.

"Well, young man, I'm afraid you'll have to go. The fact is, we should have to *higher* you before we could *hire* you;" and the clerk laughed at his witticism.

Ben naturally saw nothing to laugh at, but felt rather indignant. He stepped into the street, a little depressed at the result of his first application. But then, as he reflected, there were a great many other stores besides this, and he might have better luck next time. He walked on some distance, however, before trying again. Indeed, he had got above Bleecker Street, when his attention was arrested by a paper pasted inside of a shop-window, bearing the inscription:—

"CASH-BOYS WANTED."

Ben did not clearly understand what were the duties of a cash-boy, though he supposed they must have something to do with receiving money. Looking in through the glass door he saw boys as small as himself flitting about, and this gave him courage to enter and make an application for a place.

He entered, therefore, and walked up boldly to the first clerk he saw.

"Do you want a cash-boy?" he asked.

"Go up to that desk, Johnny," said the clerk, pointing to a desk about midway of the store. A stout gentleman stood behind it, writing something in a large book.

Ben went up, and repeated his inquiry. "Do you want a cash-boy?"

"How old are you?" asked the gentleman looking down at him.

"Ten years old."

"Have you ever been in a store?"

"No, sir."

"Do you live in the city?"

"Yes, sir."

"With your parents?"

"No, sir," said Ben, with hesitation.

"Who do you live with, then?"

"With nobody. I take care of myself."

"Humph!" The gentleman looked a little surprised, not at the idea of a boy of ten looking out for himself, for such cases are common enough in New York, but at the idea of such a well-dressed lad as Ben being in that situation.

"How long have you been your own man?" he inquired.

"I've only just begun," Ben admitted.

"Are your parents dead?"

"No, sir; they're alive."

"Then I advise you to go back to them. We don't receive any boys into our employment, who do not live with their parents."

The gentleman returned to his writing, and Ben saw that his case was hopeless. His disappointment was greater than before, for he liked the looks of the proprietor, if, as he judged, this was he. Besides, boys were wanted, and his size would be no objection, judging from the appearance of the other boys in the store. So he had been sanguine of success. Now he saw that there was an objection which he could not remove, and which would be very likely to stand in his way in other places.

CHAPTER IV

A RESTAURANT ON FULTON STREET

Ben kept on his way, looking in at the shop windows as before. He had not yet given up the idea of getting a place in a store, though he began to see that his chances of success were rather small.

The next pause he came to was before a bookstore. Here, too, there was posted on the window:—

"BOY WANTED."

Ben entered. There were two or three persons behind the counter. The oldest, a man of forty, Ben decided to be the proprietor. He walked up to him, and said, "Do you want a boy?"

"Yes," said the gentleman. "We want a boy to run of errands, and deliver papers to customers. How old are you?"

"Ten years old."

"That is rather young."

"I'm pretty strong of my age," said Ben, speaking the truth here, for he was rather larger and stouter than most boys of ten.

"That is not important, as you will not have very heavy parcels to carry. Are you well acquainted with the streets in this part of the city?"

This question was a poser, Ben thought. He was at first tempted to say yes, but decided to answer truthfully.

"No, sir," he answered.

"Do you live in the lower part of the city?"

"Yes, sir; that is, I'm going to live there."

"How long have you lived in the city?"

"I only arrived this morning," Ben confessed, reluctantly.

"Then I'm afraid you will not answer my purpose. We need a boy who is well acquainted with the city streets."

He was another disqualification. Ben left the store a little discouraged. He began to think that it would be harder work making a living than he had supposed. He would apply in two or three more stores, and, if unsuccessful, he must sell papers or black boots. Of the two he preferred selling papers. Blacking boots would soil his hands and his clothes, and, as it was possible that he might someday encounter someone from his native village, he did not like to have the report carried home that he had become a New York boot-black. He felt that his education and bringing up fitted him for something better than that. However, it was not necessary to decide this question until he had got through applying for a situation in a store.

He tried his luck again, and once was on the point of being engaged at three dollars per week, when a question as to his parents revealed the fact that he was without a guardian, and this decided the question against him.

"It's of no use," said Ben, despondently. "I might as well go back."

So he turned, and retraced his steps down Broadway. By the time he got to the City Hall Park he was quite tired. Seeing some vacant seats inside, he went in and sat down, resting his bundle on the seat beside him. He saw quite a number of street boys within the enclosure, most of them boot-blacks. As a rule, they bore the marks of their occupation not only on their clothes, but on their faces and hands as well. Some, who were a little more careful than the rest, were provided with a small square strip of carpeting, on which they kneeled when engaged in "shining up" a customer's boots. This formed a very good protection for the knees of their pantaloons. Two were even more luxurious, having chairs in which they seated their customers. Where this extra accommodation was supplied, however, a fee of ten cents was demanded, while the boot-blacks in general asked but five.

"Black your boots?" asked one boy of Ben, observing that our young adventurer's shoes were soiled.

"Yes," said Ben, "if you'll do it for nothing."

"I'll black your eye for nothing," said the other.

"Thank you," said Ben, "I won't trouble you."

Ben was rather interested in a scene which he witnessed shortly afterwards. A young man, whose appearance indicated that he was from the country, was waylaid by the boys, and finally submitted his boots to an operator.

"How much do you want?"

"Twenty-five cents," was the reply.

"Twenty-five cents!" exclaimed the customer, aghast. "You're jokin', aint you?"

"Reg'lar price, mister," was the reply.

"Why, I saw a boy blackin' boots down by the museum for ten cents."

"Maybe you did; but this is the City Hall Park. We're employed by the city, and we have to charge the reg'lar price."

"I wish I'd got my boots blacked down to the museum," said the victim, in a tone of disappointment, producing twenty-five cents, which was eagerly appropriated by the young extortioner.

"I say, Tommy, give us a treat, or we'll peach," said one of the boys.

Tom led the way to the ice-cream vender's establishment, where with reckless extravagance he ordered a penny ice-cream all round for the half-dozen boys in his company, even then making a handsome thing out of the extra pay he had obtained from his rustic patron.

By this time it was half-past two o'clock. So Ben learned from the City Hall clock. He was getting decidedly hungry. There were apple and cake stands just outside the railings, on which he could have regaled himself cheaply, but his appetite craved something more solid. There was a faint feeling, which nothing but meat could satisfy.

Ben had no idea how much a plate of meat would cost at a restaurant. He had but twenty-two cents, and whatever he got must come within that limit. Still he hoped that something could be obtained for this sum.

Where to go,—that was the question.

"Can you tell me a good place to get some dinner?" he asked of a boy, standing near him.

"Down on Nassau Street or Fulton Street," was the reply.

"Where is Fulton Street?" asked Ben, catching the last name.

"I'm goin' that way. You can go with me if you want to."

Ben readily accepted the companionship proffered, and was led past the museum, the site of which, as I have said, is now occupied by the Herald Building.

Turning down Fulton Street, Ben soon saw a restaurant, with bills of fare displayed outside.

"That's a good place," said his guide.

"Thank you," said Ben.

He scanned the bill in advance, ascertaining to his satisfaction that he could obtain a plate of roast beef for fifteen cents, and a cup of coffee for five. This would make but twenty cents, leaving him a balance of two cents.

He opened the door and entered.

There was a long table running through the centre of the apartment, from the door to the rear. On each side, against the sides of

the room, were small tables intended for four persons each. There
were but few eating, as the busy time at down-town restaurants
usually extends from twelve to half-past one, or two o'clock, and it
was now nearly three.

Ben entered and took a seat at one of the side tables, laying his
bundle on a chair beside him.

A colored waiter came up, and stood awaiting his orders.

"Give me a plate of roast beef," said Ben.

"Yes, sir. Coffee or tea?"

"Coffee."

The waiter went to the lower end of the dining-room, and called
out, "Roast beef."

After a brief delay, he returned with the article ordered, and a
cup of coffee.

There were two potatoes with the meat, and a small piece of
bread on the side of the plate. The coffee looked muddy, and not
particularly inviting.

Ben was not accustomed to the ways of restaurants, and supposed that, as in shops, immediate payment was expected.

"Here's the money—twenty cents," he said, producing the sum
named.

"Pay at the desk as you go out," said the waiter.

Ben looked up, and then for the first time noticed a man behind
a counter in the front part of the room.

At the same time the waiter produced a green ticket, bearing "20
cents" printed upon it.

Ben now addressed himself with a hearty appetite to the dinner.
The plate was dingy, and the meat neither very abundant nor very
tender. Still it can hardly be expected that for fifteen cents a large
plate of sirloin can be furnished. Ben was not in a mood to be criti-
cal. At home he would have turned up his nose at such a repast,
but hunger is very well adapted to cure one of fastidiousness. He
ate rapidly, and felt that he had seldom eaten anything so good.
He was sorry there was no more bread, the supply being exceed-
ingly limited. As for the coffee he was able to drink it, though he
did not enjoy it so well. It tasted as if there was not more than a
teaspoonful of milk in the infusion, while the flavor of the bever-
age differed strangely from the coffee he had been accustomed to
get at home.

"It isn't very good," thought Ben; and he could not help wishing
he had a cup of the good coffee his mother used to make at home.

"Have anything more?" asked the waiter, coming up to the table.

Ben looked over the bill of fare, not that he expected to get anything for the two cents that still remained to him, but because he wanted to notice the prices of different articles. His eye rested rather longingly on "Apple Dumplings." He was very fond of this dish, and his appetite was so far from being satisfied that he felt that he could have easily disposed of a plate. But the price was ten cents, and of course it was entirely beyond his means.

"Nothing more," said he, and rose from his seat.

He went up to the counter and settled his bill, and went out again into the street. He felt more comfortable than he had done, as one is very apt to feel after a good dinner, and Ben's dinner had been a good one, his appetite making up for any deficiency in the quality.

Where should he go now?

He was still tired, and did not care to wander about the streets. Besides, he had no particular place to go to. He therefore decided to walk back to the City Hall Park, and sit down on one of the benches. There would be something to see, and he was interested in watching the street boys, whose ranks he felt that he should very soon be compelled to join. His prospects did not look particularly bright, as he was not provided with means sufficient to pay for another meal. But the time had not yet come to trouble himself about that. When he got hungry again, he would probably realize his position a little more keenly.

CHAPTER V

A BEER-GARDEN IN THE BOWERY

Ben sat down again in his old seat, and occupied himself once more in looking about him. After a while he became sleepy. Besides having taken a considerable walk, he had not slept much the night before. As no one occupied the bench but himself, he thought he might as well make himself comfortable. Accordingly he laid his bundle crosswise at one end, and laid back, using it for a pillow. The visor of his cap he brought down over his eyes, so as to shield them from the afternoon sun. The seat was hard, to be sure, but his recumbent position rested him. He did not mean to go to sleep, but gradually the sounds around him became an indistinct hum; even the noise and bustle of busy Broadway, but a few feet distant, failed to ward off sleep, and in a short time he was sleeping soundly.

Of course he could not sleep in so public a place without attracting attention. Two ragged boys espied him, and held a low conference together.

"What's he got in that bundle, Jim, do you think?" asked one.

"We'd better look and see."

They went up to the bench, and touched him, to make sure that he was fast asleep. The touch did not rouse him to consciousness.

"Just lift up his head, Mike, and I'll take the bundle," said the larger of the two boys.

This was done.

"Now, let him down softly."

So the bundle was removed, and poor Ben, wandering somewhere in the land of dreams, was none the wiser. His head, deprived of its former support, now rested on the hard bench. It was not so comfortable, but he was too tired to awake. So he slept on.

Meanwhile Jim and Mike opened the bundle.

"It's a couple of shirts," said Jim.

"Is that all?" asked Mike, disappointed.

"Well, that's better than nothin'."

"Give me one of 'em."

"It's just about your size. 'Taint big enough for me."

"Then give me the two of 'em."

"What'll you give?"

"I aint got no stamps. I'll pay you a quarter when I get it."

"That don't go down," said Jim, whose confidence in his confederate's honesty was not very great. Considering the transaction in which they were now engaged, it is not surprising that there should have been a mutual distrust. Being unable to make any bargain, Jim decided to take his share of the booty round to a second-hand clothes-dealer in Chatham Street. Here, after considerable higgling, he succeeded in selling the shirt for sixteen cents, which was less than his companion had offered. However, it was cash down, and so was immediately available,—an important consideration in the present state of Jim's finances. "A bird in the hand," as he considered, "was worth two in the bush."

Jim immediately purchased a cigar with a portion of his dishonest gains, and, procuring a light, walked about in a state of high enjoyment, puffing away as coolly as a man of twice his years.

Meanwhile Ben continued to sleep, happily unconscious of the loss of his entire personal possessions. In his dreams he was at home once more, playing with his school companions. Let him sleep! He will waken soon enough to the hard realities of a street life, voluntarily undertaken, it is true, but none the less likely to bear heavily upon him.

He slept a long time. When he awoke it was six o'clock.

He sat upon his seat, and rubbed his eyes in momentary bewilderment. In his dreams he had been back again to his native village, and he could not at once recall his change of circumstances. But it all came back to him soon enough. He realized with a slight pang that he had a home no longer; that he was a penniless vagrant, for whom the hospitality of the streets alone was open. He did wish that he could sit down at the plentiful home table, and eat the well-cooked supper which was always provided; that is, if he could blot out one remembrance: when he thought of the unjust punishment that had driven him forth, his pride rose, and his determination became as stubborn as ever. I do not defend Ben in this. He was clearly wrong. The best of parents may be unintentionally unjust at times, and this is far from affording an adequate excuse for a boy to leave home. But Ben had a great deal of pride, and I am only telling you how he felt.

Our young adventurer did not at first realize the loss which he had sustained. It was at least five minutes before he thought of his bundle at all. At length, chancing to look at the seat beside him, he missed it.

"Where can it be, I wonder?" he thought, perplexed.

He looked under the bench, thinking that perhaps it had rolled off. But it need not be said that it was not to be seen.

Ben was rather disturbed. It was all he had brought from home, and constituted his entire earthly possessions.

"It must have rolled off, and been picked up by somebody," he thought; but the explanation was not calculated to bring any satisfaction. "I did not think I should fall asleep."

It occurred to him that some of the boys nearby might have seen it. So he went up to a group of boot-blacks nearby, one of whom was Jim, who had actually been concerned in the robbery. The other boys knew nothing of the affair.

"I say, boys," said Ben, "have you seen anything of my bundle?"

"What bundle, Johnny?" said Jim, who was now smoking his second cigar.

"I had a small bundle tied up in a newspaper," said Ben. "I put it under my head, and then fell asleep. Now I can't find it."

"Do you think we stole it?" said Jim, defiantly.

"Of course I don't," said Ben; "but I thought it might have slipped out, and you might have seen somebody pick it up."

"Haven't seen it, Johnny," said one of the other boys; "most likely it's stole."

"Do you think so?" asked Ben, anxiously.

"In course, you might expect it would be."

"I didn't mean to go to sleep."

"What was there in it?"

"There was two shirts."

"You've got a shirt on, aint you?"

"Yes," said Ben.

"That's all right, then. What does a feller want of a thousand shirts?"

"There's some difference between two shirts and a thousand," said Ben.

"What's the odds? I haven't got but one shirt. That's all I want. When it is wore out I'll buy a new one."

"What do you do when it gets dirty?" asked Ben, in some curiosity.

"Oh, I wash it once in two or three weeks," was the reply.

This was not exactly in accordance with Ben's ideas of neatness; but he saw that no satisfaction was likely to be obtained in this quarter, so he walked away rather depressed. It certainly hadn't been a lucky day,—this first day in the city. He had been rejected in half-a-dozen stores in his applications for employment, had spent nearly all his money, and been robbed of all his clothing except what he wore.

Again Ben began to feel an appetite. He had eaten his dinner late, but it had consisted of a plate of meat only. His funds being now reduced to two cents, he was obliged to content himself with an apple, which did something towards appeasing his appetite.

Next Ben began to consider anxiously how he was to pass the night. Having no money to spend for lodging, there seemed nothing to do but to sleep out of doors. It was warm weather, and plenty of street boys did it. But to Ben it would be a new experience, and he regarded it with some dread. He wished he could meet with Jerry Collins, his acquaintance of the morning. From him he might obtain some information that would be of service in his present strait.

Three or four hours must elapse before it would be time to go to bed. Ben hardly knew how or where to pass them. He had become tired of the park; besides, he had got over a part of his fatigue, and felt able to walk about and explore the city. He turned at a venture up Chatham Street, and was soon interested in the sights of this peculiar thoroughfare,—the shops open to the street, with half their stock in trade exposed on the sidewalk, the importunities of the traders, and the appearance of the people whom he met. It seemed very lively and picturesque to Ben, and drew away his attention from his own awkward position.

He was asked to buy by some of the traders, being promised wonderful bargains; but his penniless condition put him out of the reach of temptation.

So he wandered on until he came to the Bowery, a broad avenue, wider than Broadway, and lined by shops of a great variety, but of a grade inferior to those of its more aristocratic neighbor.

Here, also, the goods are liberally displayed on the sidewalk, and are generally labelled with low prices, which tempts many purchasers. The purchaser, however, must look carefully to the quality of the goods which he buys, or he will in many cases find the low price merely a snare and a delusion, and regret that he had not paid more liberally and bought a better article.

Later in the evening, on his return walk, Ben came to an establishment brilliant with light, from which proceeded strains of music. Looking in, he saw that it was filled with small tables, around which were seated men, women, and children. They had glasses before them from which they drank. This was a Lager Beer Hall or Garden,—an institution transplanted from Germany, and chiefly patronized by those of German birth or extraction. It seemed bright and cheerful, and our young adventurer thought it would be pleasant to go in, and spend an hour or two, listening to the music; but he was prevented by the consciousness that he had no money to spend, and might be considered an intruder.

While he was looking in wistfully, he was struck on the back; and turning, saw, to his surprise, the face of his only acquaintance in New York, Jerry Collins, the boot-black.

"I am glad to see you," he said, eagerly offering his hand, without considering that Jerry's hand, unwashed during the day, was stained with blacking. He felt so glad to meet an acquaintance, however, that he would not have minded this, even if it had occurred to him.

"The same to you," said Jerry. "Are you going in?"

"I haven't got any money," said Ben, a little ashamed of the confession.

"Well, I have, and that'll do just as well."

He took Ben by the arm, and they passed through a vestibule, and entered the main apartment, which was of large size. On one side, about half way down, was a large instrument some like an organ, from which the music proceeded. The tables were very well filled, Germans largely predominating among the guests.

"Sit down here," said Jerry.

They took seats at one of the tables. Opposite was a stout German and his wife, the latter holding a baby. Both had glasses of lager before them, and the baby was also offered a share by its mother; but, from the contortions of its face, did not appear to relish it.

"*Zwei Glass Lager*," said Jerry, to a passing attendant.

"Can you speak German?" asked Ben, surprised.

"Yaw," said Jerry; "my father was an Irishman, and my mother was a Dutchman."

Jerry's German, however, seemed to be limited, as he made no further attempts to converse in that language.

The glasses were brought. Jerry drank his down at a draught, but Ben, who had never before tasted lager, could not at once become reconciled to its bitter taste.

"Don't you like it?" asked Jerry.

"Not very much," said Ben.

"Then I'll finish it for you;" and he suited the action to the word.

Besides the lager a few plain cakes were sold, but nothing more substantial. Evidently the beer was the great attraction. Ben could not help observing, with some surprise, that, though everybody was drinking, there was not the slightest disturbance, or want of decorum, or drunkenness. The music, which was furnished at intervals, was of very good quality, and was listened to with attention.

"I was goin' to Tony Pastor's to-night," said Jerry, "if I hadn't met you."

"What sort of a place is that?" asked Ben.

"Oh, it's a bully place—lots of fun. You must go there some time."

"I think I will," answered Ben, mentally adding, "if I ever have money enough."

Here the music struck up, and they stopped to listen to it. When this was over, Jerry proposed to go out. Ben would have been willing to stay longer; but he saw that his companion did not care so much for the music as himself, and he did not wish to lose sight of him. To be alone in a great city, particularly under Ben's circumstances, is not very pleasant, and our young adventurer determined to stick to his new acquaintance, who, though rough in his manners, had yet seemed inclined to be friendly, and Ben felt sadly in need of a friend.

CHAPTER VI

THE BURNING BALES

"Where are you going to sleep to-night?" asked Ben, introducing a subject which had given him some anxiety.

"I don't know," said Jerry, carelessly. "I'll find a place somewhere."

"I'll go with you, if you'll let me," said Ben.

"In course I will."

"I haven't got any money."

"What's the odds? They don't charge nothin' at the hotel where I stop."

"What time do you go to bed?"

"Most any time. Do you feel sleepy?"

"Rather. I didn't sleep much last night."

"Well, we'll go and find a place now. How'd you like sleepin' on cotton-bales?"

"I think that would be comfortable."

"There's a pile of bales down on the pier, where the New Orleans steamers come in. Maybe we could get a chance there."

"All right. Where is it?"

"Pier 8, North River. It'll take us twenty minutes, or maybe half an hour, to go there."

"Let us go," said Ben.

He felt relieved at the idea of so comfortable a bed as a cotton-bale, and was anxious to get stowed away for the night.

The two boys struck across to Broadway, and followed that street down past Trinity Church, turning down the first street beyond. Rector Street, notwithstanding its clerical name, is far from an attractive street. Just in the rear of the great church, and extending down to the wharves, is a collection of miserable dwellings, occupied by tenants upon whom the near presence of the sanctuary appears to produce little impression of a salutary character. Ben looked about him in ill-concealed disgust. He neither fancied the neighborhood, nor the people whom he met. But the Island is very narrow just here, and he had not far to walk to West Street, which runs along the edge of Manhattan Island, and is lined with wharves. Jerry, of course, did not mind the surroundings. He was too well used to them to care.

They brought out opposite the pier.

"There it is," said Jerry.

Ben saw a pile of cotton-bales heaped up on the wharf in front. Just behind them was a gate, and over it the sign of the New Orleans Company.

"I should think somebody would steal the bales," said Ben. "Are they left out here all night?"

"There's a watchman round here somewhere," said Jerry. "He stays here all night to guard the bales."

"Will he let us sleep here?"

"I don't know," said Jerry. "We'll creep in, when he isn't looking."

The watchman was sitting down, leaning his back against one of the bales. A short pipe was in his mouth, and he seemed to be enjoying his smoke. This was contrary to orders, for the cotton being combustible might easily catch fire; but this man, supposing that he would not be detected, indulged himself in the forbidden luxury.

"Now creep along softly," said Jerry.

The latter, being barefooted, had an advantage over Ben, but our young adventurer crept after him as softly as he could. Jerry found a bale screened from observation by the higher piles on each side, where he thought they could sleep unobserved. Following his lead, Ben stretched himself out upon it.

The watchman was too busily occupied with his pipe to detect any noise.

"Aint it comfortable?" whispered Jerry.

"Yes," said Ben, in the same low tone.

"I wouldn't ask for nothin' better," said Jerry.

Ben was not so sure about that; but then he had not slept out hundreds of nights, like Jerry, in old wagons, or on door-steps, or wherever else he could; so he had a different standard of comparison.

He could not immediately go to sleep. He was tired, it was true, but his mind was busy. It was only twelve hours since he had landed in the city, but it had been an eventful twelve hours. He understood his position a little better now, and how much he had undertaken, in boldly leaving home at ten years of age, and taking upon himself the task of earning his living.

If he had known what was before him, would he have left home at all?

Ben was not sure about this. He did own to himself, however, that he was disappointed. The city had not proved the paradise he had expected. Instead of finding shopkeepers eager to secure his services, he had found himself uniformly rejected. He began to suspect that it was rather early to begin the world at ten years of age. Then again, though he was angry with his father, he had no cause of complaint against his mother. She had been uniformly kind and gentle, and he found it hard to keep back the tears when he thought how she would be distressed at his running away. He had not thought of that in the heat of his first anger, but he thought of it now. How would she feel if she knew where he was at this moment, resting on a cotton-bale, on a city wharf, penniless and without a friend in the great city, except the ragged boy who was already asleep at his side? She would feel badly, Ben knew that, and he half regretted having been so precipitate in his action. He could remedy it all, and relieve his mother's heart by going back. But here Ben's pride came in. To go back would be to acknowledge himself wrong; it would be a virtual confession of failure, and, moreover, knowing his father's sternness, he knew that he would be severely punished. Unfortunately for Ben, his father had a stern, unforgiving disposition, that never made allowances for the impulses of boyhood. He had never condescended to study his own son, and the method of training he had adopted with him was in some respects very pernicious. His system hardened, instead of softening, and prejudiced Ben against what was right, maddening him with a sense of injustice, and so preventing his being influenced towards good. Of course, all this did not justify Ben in running away from home. The thought of his mother ought to have been sufficient to have kept him from any such step. But it was necessary to be stated, in order that my readers might better understand what sort of a boy Ben was.

So, in spite of his half relenting, Ben determined that he would not go home at all events. Whatever hardships lay before him in the new life which he had adopted, he resolved to stand them as well as he could. Indeed, however much he might desire to retrace his steps, he had no money to carry him back, nor could he obtain any unless he should write home for it, and this again would be humiliating. Ben's last thought, then, as he sank to sleep, was, that he would stick to New York, and get his living somehow, even if he had to black boots for a living.

At the end of an hour, both boys were fast asleep. The watchman, after smoking his pipe, got up, and paced up and down the wharf drowsily. He did not happen to observe the young sleepers. If he had done so, he would undoubtedly have shaken them roughly, and ordered them off. It was rather fortunate that neither Ben nor his companion were in the habit of snoring, as this would at once have betrayed their presence, even to the negligent watchman.

After a while the watchman bethought himself again of his pipe, and, filling the bowl with tobacco, lighted it. Then, with the most culpable carelessness, he half reclined on one of the bales and "took comfort." Not having prepared himself for the vigils of the night by repose during the day, he began to feel uncommonly drowsy. The whiffs came less and less frequently, until at last the pipe fell from his lips, and he fell back fast asleep. The burning contents of the pipe fell on the bale, and gradually worked their way down into the interior. Here the mischief soon spread. What followed may easily be imagined.

Ben was aroused from his sleep by a confused outcry. He rubbed his eyes to see what was the matter. There was something stifling and suffocating in the atmosphere, which caused him to choke as he breathed. As he became more awake, he realized that the cotton-bales, among which he had taken refuge, were on fire. He became alarmed, and shook Jerry energetically.

"What's up?" said Jerry, drowsily. "I aint done nothin'. You can't take me up."

"Jerry, wake up; the bales are on fire," said Ben.

"I thought 'twas a copp," said Jerry, rousing, and at a glance understanding the position of affairs. "Let's get out of this."

That was not quite so easy. There was fire on all sides, and they must rush through it at some risk. However, it was every moment getting worse, and there was no chance for delay.

"Foller me," said Jerry, and he dashed through, closely pursued by Ben.

By this time quite a crowd of men and boys had gathered around the burning bales.

When the two boys rushed out, there was a general exclamation of surprise. Then one burly man caught Jerry by the arm, and said, "Here's the young villain that set the bales on fire."

"Let me alone, will you?" said Jerry. "Yer grandmother set it on fire, more likely."

No sooner was Jerry seized, than another man caught hold of Ben, and forcibly detained him.

"I've got the other," he said.

"Now, you young rascal, tell me how you did it," said the first.

"Was you smokin'?"

"No, I wasn't," said Jerry, shortly. "I was sleepin' along of this other boy."

"What made you come here to sleep?"

"'Cause we hadn't no other bed."

"Are you sure you wasn't smoking?"

"Look here," said Jerry, contemptuously, "you must think I'm a fool, to go and set my own bed on fire."

"That's true," said a bystander. "It wouldn't be very likely."

"Who did it, then?" asked the stout man, suspiciously.

"It's the watchman. I seed him smokin' when I turned in."

"Where is he now?"

Search was made for the watchman, but he had disappeared. Awaking to a consciousness of what mischief he had caused through his carelessness, he had slipped away in the confusion, and was not likely to return.

"The boy tells the truth," said one of the crowd. "I saw the watchman smoking myself. No doubt the fire caught from his pipe. The boys are innocent. Better let them go."

The two custodians of Jerry and Ben released their hold, and they gladly availed themselves of the opportunity to remove themselves to a safer distance from their late bedchamber.

Two fire-engines came thundering up, and streams of water were directed effectively at the burning bales. The flames were extinguished, but not till considerable damage had been done.

As the two boys watched the contest between the flames and the engines, from a safe distance, they heard the sonorous clang of the bell in the church-tower, ringing out twelve o'clock.

CHAPTER VII

BEN'S TEMPTATION

"Jest my luck!" complained Jerry. "Why couldn't the fire have waited till mornin'?"

"We might have burned up," said Ben, who was considerably impressed by his narrow escape.

"Only we didn't," said Jerry. "We'll have to try another hotel for the rest of the night."

"Where shall we go?"

"We may find a hay-barge down to the pier at the foot of Franklin Street."

"Is it far?"

"Not very."

"Let us go then."

So the boys walked along the street until they came to the pier referred to. There was a barge loaded with hay, lying alongside the wharf. Jerry speedily provided himself with a resting-place upon it, and Ben followed his example. It proved to be quite as comfortable, if not more so, than their former bed, and both boys were soon asleep. How long he slept Ben did not know, but he was roused to consciousness by a rude shake.

"Wake up there!" said a voice.

Ben opened his eyes, and saw a laboring man bending over him.

"Is it time to get up?" he inquired, hardly conscious where he was.

"I should think it was, particularly as you haven't paid for your lodging."

"Where's Jerry?" asked Ben, missing the boot-black.

The fact was, that Jerry, whose business required him to be astir early, had been gone over an hour. He had not felt it necessary to wake up Ben, knowing that the latter had nothing in particular to call him up.

"I don't know anything about Jerry. You'd better be going home, young 'un. Take my advice, and don't stay out another night."

He evidently thought that Ben was a truant from home, as his dress would hardly class him among the homeless boys who slept out from necessity.

Ben scrambled upon the pier, and took a cross street up towards Broadway. He had slept off his fatigue, and the natural appetite of a healthy boy began to assert itself. It was rather uncomfortable to reflect that he was penniless, and had no means of buying a breakfast. He had meant to ask Jerry's advice, as to some occupation by which he could earn a little money, and felt disappointed that his companion had gone away before he waked up. His appetite was the greater because he had been limited to a single apple for supper.

Where to go he did not know. One place was as good as another. It was a strange sensation to Ben to feel the cravings of appetite, with nothing to satisfy it. All his life he had been accustomed to a good home, where his wants were plentifully provided for. He had never had any anxiety about the supply of his daily wants. In the city there were hundreds of boys younger than he, who, rising in the morning, knew not where their meals were to come from, or whether they were to have any; but this had never been his case.

"I am young and strong," thought Ben. "Why can't I find something to do?"

His greatest anxiety was to work, and earn his living somehow; but how did not seem clear. Even if he were willing to turn bootblack, he had no box nor brush, and had some doubts whether he should at first possess the requisite skill. Selling papers struck him more favorably; but here again the want of capital would be an objection.

So, in a very perplexed frame of mind, our young adventurer went on his way, and after a while caught sight of the upper end of the City Hall Park. Here he felt himself at home, and, entering, looked among the dozens of boys who were plying their work to see if he could not find his acquaintance Jerry. But here he was unsuccessful. Jerry's business stand was near the Cortlandt Street pier.

Hour after hour passed, and Ben became more and more hungry and dispirited. He felt thoroughly helpless. There seemed to be nothing that he could do. He began to be faint, and his head ached. One o'clock found him on Nassau Street, near the corner of Fulton. There was a stand for the sale of cakes and pies located here, presided over by an old woman, of somewhat ample dimensions. This stall had a fascination for poor Ben. He had such a craving for food that he could not take his eyes off the tempting pile of cakes which were heaped up before him. It seemed to him that he should be perfectly happy if he could be permitted to eat all he wanted of them.

Ben knew that it was wrong to steal. He had never in his life taken what did not belong to him, which is more than many boys can say, who have been brought up even more comfortably than he. But the temptation now was very strong. He knew it was not right; but he was not without excuse. Watching his opportunity, he put his hand out quickly, and, seizing a couple of pies, stowed them away hastily in his pocket, and was about moving off to eat them in some place where he would not be observed. But though the owner of the stolen articles had not observed the theft, there was a boy hanging about the stall, possibly with the same object in view, who did see it.

"He's got some of your pies, old lady," said the young detective.

The old woman looked round, and though the pies were in Ben's pocket there was a telltale in his face which betrayed him.

"Put back them pies, you young thafe!" said the angry pie-merchant. "Aint you ashamed of yerself to rob a poor widdy, that has hard work to support herself and her childers,—you that's dressed like a gentleman, and ought to know better?"

"Give it to him, old lady," said the hard-hearted young vagabond, who had exposed Ben's iniquity.

As for Ben, he had not a word to say. In spite of his hunger, he was overwhelmed with confusion at having actually attempted to steal, and been caught in the act. He was by no means a model boy; but apart from anything which he had been taught in the Sunday school, he considered stealing mean and discreditable, and yet he had been led into it. What would his friends at home think of it, if they should ever hear of it? So, as I said, he stood without a word to say in his defense, mechanically replacing the pies on the stall.

"I say, old lady, you'd orter give me a pie for tellin' you," said the informer.

"You'd have done the same, you young imp, if you'd had the chance," answered the pie-vender, with more truth than gratitude. "Clear out, the whole on ye. I've had trouble enough with ye."

Ben moved off, thankful to get off so well. He had feared that he might be handed over to the police, and this would have been the crowning disgrace.

But the old woman seemed satisfied with the restoration of her property, and the expression of her indignation. The attempt upon her stock she regarded with very little surprise, having suffered more than once before in a similar way.

But there was another spectator of the scene, whose attention had been drawn to the neat attire and respectable appearance of Ben. He saw that he differed considerably from the ordinary run of street boys. He noticed also the flush on the boy's cheek when he was detected, and judged that this was his first offence. Something out of the common way must have driven him to the act. He felt impelled to follow Ben, and learn what that something was. I may as well state here that he was a young man of twenty-five or thereabouts, a reporter on one or more of the great morning papers. He, like Ben, had come to the city in search of employment, and before he secured it had suffered more hardships and privations than he liked to remember. He was now earning a modest income, sufficient to provide for his wants, and leave a surplus over. He had seen much of suffering and much of crime in his daily walks about the city, but his heart had not become hardened, nor his sympathies blunted. He gave more in proportion to his means than many rich men who have a reputation for benevolence.

Ben had walked but a few steps, when he felt a hand upon his shoulder.

Looking round hastily, he met the gaze of the young man. He had thought at first it might be a policeman, and he felt relieved when he saw his mistake.

"You are the boy who just now took a couple of pies from a stall?" said the reporter.

"Yes," said Ben, hesitatingly, his face crimsoning as he spoke.

"Do you mind telling me why you did so?"

There was something in his tone which reassured Ben, and he determined to tell the truth frankly.

"I have eaten nothing to-day," he said.

"You never took anything before?"

"No," said Ben, quickly.

"I suppose you had no money to buy with?"

"No, I had not."

"How does it happen that a boy as well dressed as you are, are in such a position?"

"I would rather not tell," said Ben.

"Have you run away from home?"

"Yes; I had a good reason," he added, quickly.

"What do you propose to do? You must earn your living in some way, or starve."

"I thought I might get a place in a store; but I have tried half a dozen, and they won't take me."

"No, your chance will be small, unless you can bring good references. But you must be hungry."

"I am," Ben admitted.

"That can be remedied, at all events. I am just going to get some dinner; will you go with me?"

"I have no money."

"I have, and that will answer the purpose for this time. We will go back to Fulton Street."

Ben turned back thankfully, and with his companion entered the very restaurant in which he had dined the day before.

"If you are faint, soup will be the best thing for you to begin on," said the young man; and he gave an order to the waiter.

Nothing had ever seemed more delicious to Ben than that soup. When he had done justice to it, a plate of beefsteak awaited him, which also received his attention. Then he was asked to select some dessert.

"I am afraid you are spending too much for me," he said.

"Don't be afraid of that; I am glad that you have a good appetite."

At length the dinner was over. Ben felt decidedly better. His despondency had vanished, and the world again seemed bright to him. It is hard to be cheerful, or take bright views of life on an empty stomach, as many have learned beside our young adventurer.

"Now," said his new-found friend, "I have a few minutes to spare. Suppose we talk over your plans and prospects, and see if we can find anything for you to do."

"Thank you," said Ben; "I wish you would give me your advice."

"My advice is that you return to your home, if you have one," said the reporter.

Ben shook his head.

"I don't want to do that," he answered.

"I don't, of course, know what is your objection to this, which seems to me the best course. Putting it aside, however, we will consider what you can do here to earn your living."

"That is what I want to do."

"How would you like selling papers?"

"I think I should like it," said Ben; "but I have no money to buy any."

"It doesn't require a very large capital. I will lend you, or give you, the small amount which will be necessary. However, you mustn't expect to make a very large income."

"If I can make enough to live on, I won't care," said Ben.

He had at first aimed higher; but his short residence in the city taught him that he would be fortunate to meet his expenses. There are a good many besides Ben who have found their early expectations of success considerably modified by experience.

"Let me see. It is half-past one o'clock," said the reporter, drawing out his watch. "You had better lay in a supply of 'Expresses' and 'Evening Posts,' and take a good stand somewhere, and do your best with them. As you are inexperienced in the business it will be well to take a small supply at first, or you might get 'stuck.'"

"That's so."

"You must not lay in more than you can sell."

"Where can I get the papers?"

"I will go with you to the newspaper offices, and buy you half a dozen of each. If you succeed in selling them, you can buy more. To-morrow you can lay in some of the morning papers, the 'Herald,' 'World,' 'Tribune,' or 'Times.' It will be well also to have a few 'Suns' for those who do not care to pay for the higher-priced papers."

"Thank you," said Ben, who was eager to begin his business career.

They rose from the table, and set out for the offices of the two evening papers whose names have been mentioned.

CHAPTER VIII

BEN COMMENCES HIS BUSINESS CAREER

Ben soon took his stand in the street, with a roll of papers under his arm, supplied by the generosity of his new acquaintance. It was rather a trying ordeal for a country boy, new to the city and its ways. But Ben was not bashful. He was not a timid boy, but was fully able to push his way. So, glancing at the telegraphic headings, he began to call out the news in a business-like way. He had already taken notice of how the other newsboys acted, and therefore was at no loss how to proceed.

He met with very fair success, selling out the twelve papers which had been bought for him, in a comparatively short time. It might have been that the fact that he was neater and better dressed operated in his favor. At any rate, though a new hand, he succeeded better than those who were older in the business.

But his neat dress operated to his disadvantage in another quarter. His business rivals, who were, with scarcely an exception, dressed with no great pretensions to style or neatness, looked upon the interloper with a jealous eye. They regarded him as "stuck up," in virtue of his superior dress, and were indignant to find their sales affected by his competition.

"Who's he? Ever seen him afore?" asked Tim Banks of a newsboy at his side.

"No; he's a new chap."

"What business has he got to come here and steal away our trade, I'd like to know?" continued Tim, eying Ben with no friendly glance.

At that moment a gentleman, passing Tim, bought an "Evening Post" of Ben. It was the third paper that Ben had sold since Tim had effected a sale. This naturally increased his indignation.

"He's puttin' on airs just because he's got good clo'es," said the other newsboy, who shared Tim's feelings on the subject.

"Let's shove him out," suggested Tim.

"All right."

Tim, who was a boy of twelve, with a shock head, which looked as if it had never been combed, and a suit of clothes which bore the marks of severe usage, advanced to Ben, closely followed by his confederate, who had agreed to back him.

Ben had just sold his last paper when the two approached him. He did not understand their object until Tim, swaggering up to him, said offensively, "You'd better clear out; you aint wanted here."

Ben turned and faced his ragged opponent with intrepidity.

"Why aint I wanted here?" he inquired, without manifesting the least symptom of alarm.

Tim rather anticipated that Ben would show the white feather, and was a little surprised at his calmness.

"Cause yer aint, that's why," he answered.

"If you don't like my company, you can go somewhere else," said Ben.

"This is *my* place," said Tim. "You aint got no right to push in."

"If it's your place, how much did you pay for it?" asked Ben. "I thought that the sidewalk was free to all."

"You aint got no right to interfere with my business."

"I didn't know that I had interfered with it."

"Well, you have. I aint sold more'n half as many papers since you've been here."

"You've got the same chance as I have," said Ben. "I didn't tell them not to buy of you."

"Well, you aint wanted here, and you'd better make tracks," said Tim, who considered this the best argument of all.

"Suppose I don't," said Ben.

"Then I'll give you a lickin'."

Ben surveyed the boy who uttered this threat, in the same manner that a general would examine an opposing force, with a view to ascertain his strength and ability to cope with him. It was clear that Tim was taller than himself, and doubtless older. As to being stronger, Ben did not feel so positive. He was himself well and compactly made, and strong of his age. He did not relish the idea of being imposed upon, and prepared to resist any encroachment upon his rights. He did not believe that Tim had any right to order him off. He felt that the sidewalk was just as free to him as to any other boy, and he made up his mind to assert and maintain his right.

"If you want to give me a licking, just try it," he said. "I've got just as much right to stand here and sell papers as you have, and I'm going to do it."

"You needn't be so stuck up jest because you've got good clo'es on."

"If they are good, I can't help it," said Ben. "They're all I have, and they won't be good long."

"Maybe I could get good clo'es if I'd steal em," said Tim.

"Do you mean to say I stole these?" retorted Ben, angrily. He had no sooner said it, however, than he thought of the pies which he should have stolen if he had not been detected, and his face flushed. Luckily Tim did not know why his words produced an effect upon Ben, or he would have followed up his attack.

"Yes, I do," said Tim.

"Then you judge me by yourself," said Ben, "that's all I've got to say."

"Say that ag'in," said Tim, menacingly.

"So I will, if you want to hear it. You judge me by yourself."

"I'll give you a lickin'."

"You've said that before."

Tim was not particularly brave. Still Ben was a smaller boy, and besides he had a friend at hand to back him, so he concluded that it would be safe to venture. Doubling up a dirty fist, he struck out, intending to hit Ben in the face; but our young adventurer was on his guard, and fended off the blow with his arms.

"Will yer go now?" demanded Tim, pausing after his attack.

"Why should I?"

"If you don't I'll give you another lick."

"I can stand it, if it isn't any worse than that."

Tim was spurred by this to renew the assault. He tried to throw his arms around Ben, and lift him from the ground, which would enable him to throw him with greater ease. But Ben was wary, and experienced in this mode of warfare, having often had scuffles in fun with his school-fellows. He evaded Tim's grasp, therefore, and dealt him a blow in the breast, which made Tim stagger back. He began to realize that Ben, though a smaller boy, was a formidable opponent, and regretted that he had undertaken a contest with him. He was constrained to appeal to his companion for assistance.

"Just lend a hand, Jack, and we'll give it to him."

"So you have to ask help," said Ben, scornfully, "though you're bigger than I am."

"I could lick yer well enough alone," said Tim, "but you've been interferin' with Jack's business, as well as mine."

Jack responded to his friend's appeal, and the two advanced to the assault of Ben. Of course all this took place much more quickly than it has taken to describe it. The contest commenced, and our young adventurer would have got the worst of it, if help had not arrived. Though a match for either of the boys singly, he could not be expected to cope with both at a time, especially as he was smaller than either.

Tim found himself seized forcibly by the arm, just as he was about to level a blow at Ben. Looking up, he met the glance of another newsboy, a boy of fourteen, who was known among his comrades as "Rough and Ready." This boy was stout and strong, and was generally liked by those of his class for his generous qualities, as well as respected for his physical strength, which he was always ready to exert in defense of a weaker boy.

"What's all this, Tim?" he demanded. "Aint you ashamed, the two of you, to pitch into a smaller boy?"

"He aint got no business here," said Tim, doggedly.

"Why not?"

"He's takin' away all our trade."

"Hasn't he just as much right to sell papers as you?"

"He can go somewhere else."

"So can you."

"He's a new boy. This is the first day he's sold papers."

"Then you ought to be able to keep up with him. What's your name, young un?"

This question was, of course, addressed to Ben.

"Ben," answered our young hero. He did not think it necessary to mention his other name, especially as, having run away from home, he had a vague idea that it might lead to his discovery.

"Well, Ben, go ahead and sell your papers. I'll see that you have fair play."

"Thank you," said Ben. "I'm not afraid of either of them."

"Both of them might be too much for you."

"I don't want to interfere with their business. They've got just as good a chance to sell as I have."

"Of course they have. Is this your first day?"

"Yes."

"How many papers have you sold?"

"Six 'Posts' and six 'Expresses.'"

"That's pretty good for a beginning. Are you going to get some more?"

"Yes, I was just going into the office when that boy," pointing to Tim, "tried to drive me off."

"He won't do it again. Come in with me. I'm going to buy some papers too."

"What's your name?" asked Ben. "I like you; you're not mean, like those fellows."

"My name is Rufus, but the boys call me Rough and Ready."

"Where do you live,—at the Newsboys' Lodging House?"

"No, I live in Leonard Street. I've got a mother and a little sister. I live with them."

"Have you got a father?"

"No, that is, not a real father. I've got a step-father; but he's worse than none, for he is loafing round most of the time, and spends all the money he can get on drink. If it wasn't for me, he'd treat mother worse than he does. How long have you been in New York?"

"Only a day or two," said Ben.

"Where are you living?"

"Anywhere I can. I haven't got any place."

"Where did you sleep last night?"

"In a hay-barge, at one of the piers, along with a boot-black named Jerry. That was the first night I ever slept out."

"How did you like it?"

"I think I'd prefer a bed," said Ben.

"You can get one at the Lodge for six cents."

"I didn't have six cents last night."

"They'll trust you there, and you can pay next time."

"Where is the Lodging House?"

"It's on the corner of this street and Fulton," said Rough and Ready. "I'll show it to you, if you want me to."

"I'd like to have you. I'd rather pay six cents than sleep out again."

By this time they reached the office of the "Express," and, entering, purchased a supply of papers. He was about to invest his whole capital, but, by the advice of his companion, bought only eight copies, as by the time these were disposed of a later edition would be out, which of course would be more salable.

CHAPTER IX

SCENES AT THE NEWSBOYS' LODGING HOUSE

It will be unnecessary to give in detail the record of Ben's sales. He succeeded, because he was in earnest, and he was in earnest, because his own experience in the early part of the day had revealed to him how uncomfortable it was to be without money or friends in a large city. At seven o'clock, on counting over his money, he found that he had a dollar and twelve cents. Of this sum he had received half a dollar from the friendly reporter, to start him in business. This left sixty-two cents as his net profits for the afternoon's work. Ben felt proud of it, for it was the first money he had ever earned. His confidence came back to him, and he thought he saw his way clear to earning his own living.

Although the reporter had not exacted repayment, Ben determined to lay aside fifty cents for that purpose. Of the remaining sixty-two, a part must be saved as a fund for the purchase of papers the next morning. Probably thirty cents would be sufficient for this, as, after selling out those first purchased, he would have money for a new supply. This would leave him thirty-two cents to pay for his supper, lodging, and breakfast. Ben would not have seen his way to accomplish all this for so small a sum, if he had not been told that at the Newsboys' Lodge the regular charge was six cents for each meal, and the same for lodging. This would make but eighteen cents, leaving him a surplus of fourteen. On inquiry, however, he ascertained that it was already past the hour for supper at the Lodge, and therefore went into the restaurant, on Fulton Street, where he ordered a cup of coffee, and a plate of tea-biscuit. These cost ten cents. Finding his appetite still unsatisfied, he ordered another plate of biscuit, which carried up the expense of his supper to fifteen cents. This left seventeen cents for lodging and breakfast.

After supper, he went out into the street once more, and walked about for some time, until he began to feel tired, when he turned his steps towards the Newsboys' Lodge. This institution occupied at that time the two upper stories of the building at the corner of Nassau and Fulton Streets. On the first floor was the office of the

"Daily Sun." The entrance to the Lodge was on Fulton Street. Ben went up a steep and narrow staircase, and kept mounting up until he reached the sixth floor. Here to the left he saw a door partially opened, through which he could see a considerable number of boys, whose appearance indicated that they belonged to the class known as street boys. He pushed the door open and entered. He found himself in a spacious, but low-studded apartment, abundantly lighted by rows of windows on two sides. At the end nearest the door was a raised platform, on which stood a small melodeon, which was used at the Sunday-evening meetings. There were rows of benches in the centre of the apartment for the boys.

A stout, pleasant-looking man, who proved to be Mr. O'Connor, the superintendent, advanced to meet Ben, whom he at once recognized as a new-comer.

"Is this the Newsboys' Lodge?" asked Ben.

"Yes," said the superintendent; "do you wish to stop with us?"

"I should like to sleep here to-night," said Ben.

"You are quite welcome."

"How much do you charge?"

"Our charge is six cents."

"Here is the money," said Ben, drawing it from his vest-pocket.

"What is your name?"

"Benjamin."

"And your other name?"

"Brandon," answered Ben, with some hesitation.

"What do you do for a living?"

"I am selling papers."

"Well, we will assign you a bed."

"Where are the beds?" asked Ben, looking about him.

"They are on the floor below. Any of the boys will go down and show you when you get ready to retire."

"Can I get breakfast here in the morning?" inquired Ben.

"Certainly. We charge the same as for lodging."

Ben handed over six cents additional, and congratulated himself that he was not as badly off as the night before, being sure of a comfortable bed, and a breakfast in the morning.

"What are those for?" he asked, pointing to a row of drawers or lockers on the sides of the apartment near the floor.

"Boys who have any extra clothing, or any articles which they value, are allowed to use them. Here they are safe, as they can be locked. We will assign you one if you wish."

"I have nothing to put away," said Ben. "I had a little bundle of clothes; but they were stolen from me while I was lying asleep on a bench in the City Hall Park."

"I suppose you don't know who took them?"

"No," said Ben; "but I think it was some of the boys that were blacking boots near me.—That boy's got one of them on," he said, suddenly, in an excited tone, pointing out Mike, the younger of the two boys who had appropriated his bundle. Mike had locked up his own shirt, which was considerably the worse for wear, and put on Ben's, which gave him a decidedly neater appearance than before. He had thought himself perfectly safe in doing so, not dreaming that he would be brought face to face with the true owner in the Lodge.

"What makes you think it is yours?" asked Mr. O'Connor.

"It is cut like mine," said Ben. "Besides I remember getting a large spot of ink on one of the sleeves, which would not wash out. There it is, on the left arm."

As Ben had said, there was a faint bluish spot on the sleeve of the shirt. This made Ben's story a plausible one, though not conclusive. The superintendent decided to inquire of Mike about the matter, and see what explanation he could give.

"Mike Rafferty," he said, in a tone of authority, "come here; I want you."

Mike came forward, but when he saw Ben, whom he recognized, he felt a little taken aback. But he had not been brought up in the streets for nothing. His embarrassment was only momentary. He determined to brazen it out, and swear, if anything was said about the shirt, that it was his own lawful property.

"I see you've got a new shirt on, Mike," said Mr. O'Connor.

"Yes, sir," said Mike.

"Where did you get it?"

"Where would I get it?" said Mike. "I bought it yesterday."

"Where did you buy it?"

"Round in Baxter Street," said Mike, confidently.

"It is a pretty good shirt for Baxter Street," remarked Mr. O'Connor. "How much did you pay for it?"

"Fifty cents," answered Mike, glibly.

"This may all be true, Mike," said the superintendent; "but I am not certain about it. This boy here says it is his shirt, and he thinks that you stole it from him while he was lying asleep in City Hall Park yesterday."

"It's a lie he's tellin', sir," said Mike. "I never seed him afore."

Here seemed to be a conflict of evidence. Of the two Ben seemed the more likely to tell the truth. Still it was possible that he might be mistaken, and Mike might be right after all.

"Have you any other proof that the shirt is yours?" asked Mr. O'Connor, turning to Ben.

"Yes," said Ben, "my name is marked on the shirt, just below the waist."

"We can settle the matter quickly then. Mike, pull out the shirt, so that we can see it."

Mike made some objection, which was quickly overruled. The shirt, being examined, bore the name of "Benj. Brandon," just as Ben had said.

"The shirt is yours," said the superintendent to Ben.

"Now, Mike, what did you mean by telling me that lie? It was bad enough to steal, without adding a lie besides."

"I bought the shirt in Baxter Street," persisted Mike, unblushingly.

"Then how do you account for his name on it?"

"Maybe he sold it to the man I bought it of."

"I didn't sell it at all," said Ben.

"Was that all you had taken?"

"No," said Ben. "There was another shirt besides."

"Do you know anything about it, Mike?"

"No, I don't," said Mike.

"I don't know whether you are telling the truth or not," said the superintendent; "but at any rate you must take this off, and give it to the right owner."

"And will he pay me the fifty cents?" asked Mike.

"I don't think you bought it at all; but if you did, you can prove it by the man you bought it of. If you can do that, I will see that the money is refunded to you."

There was one strong reason for discrediting Mike's story. These Baxter-Street shops are often the receptacles of stolen goods. As their identification might bring the dealers into trouble, they are very careful, as soon as an article comes into their possession, to obliterate all the marks of former ownership. It was hardly likely that they would suffer a shirt to go out of their hands so plainly marked as was the case in the present instance. Mr. O'Connor, of course, knew this, and accordingly had very little fear that he was doing injustice to Mike in ordering him to make restitution to Ben.

Mike was forced, considerably against his will, to take off the new shirt, and put on his old ragged one. But the former was no longer as clean as formerly.

"Where can I get it washed?" asked Ben.

"You can wash it yourself, in the wash-room, or you can carry it to a laundry, as some of the boys do, if you are willing to pay for it."

"I think I would rather carry it to a laundry," said Ben, who doubted strongly his ability to wash the shirt so as to improve its appearance. The superintendent accordingly gave him the direction to one of these establishments.

Opposite the room which he had entered was a smaller room used by the boys as a gymnasium. Ben looked into it, and determined to use it on some future occasion. He next went into the wash-room. Here he saw two or three boys, stripped to the waist, engaged in washing out their shirts. Being provided with but a single one each, they left them to dry over night while they were in bed, and could dispense with them. Ben wondered how they managed about ironing them; but he soon found that with these amateur laundresses ironing was not considered necessary. They are put on rough-dry in the morning, and so worn until they are considered dirty enough for another purification.

Ben looked about him with interest. The boys were chatting in an animated manner, detailing their experiences during the day, or "chaffing" each other in a style peculiar to themselves.

"Say, Jim," said one, "didn't I see you at the Grand Opera last night?"

"Yes, of course you did," said Jim. "I was in a private box along with the mayor. I had a di'mond pin in the bosom of my shirt."

"Yes, I seed you through my opera-glass. What have you done with your di'mond pin?"

"Do you think I'd bring it here to be stole? No, I keep it in my safe, along of my other valooables."

Ben listened in amusement, and thought that Jim would have cut rather a singular figure in the mayor's box.

Several boys, who had gone barefoot, were washing their feet, that being required previous to going to bed. This is necessary; otherwise the clean bed-clothes would be so soiled as to require daily washing.

The boys seemed to be having a good time, and then, though he was unacquainted with any of them, felt that it was much pleasanter to be here, in a social atmosphere, than wandering around by himself in the dark and lonely streets. He observed one thing with surprise, that the boys refrained from profane or vulgar speech, though they were by no means so particular in the street during the day. This is, however, a rule strictly enforced by the superintendent, and, if not complied with, the offender is denied the privilege of the Lodging House.

After a while Ben expressed a desire to go to bed, and in company with one of the boys descended to a room equally large, in the story below, where over a hundred single beds were arranged in tiers, in a manner very similar to the berths of a steamboat. Ben was agreeably surprised by the neat and comfortable appearance of these beds. He felt that he should be nearly as well provided for as at home. Quickly undressing himself, he jumped into the bed assigned him, and in a few minutes was fast asleep.

CHAPTER X

FURTHER EXPERIENCES

Ben had a comfortable night's rest, and when he awoke in the morning he felt that a bed at the Newsboys' Lodge was considerably better than a bale of cotton, or a hay-barge. At an early hour in the morning the boys were called, and began to tumble out in all directions, interchanging, as they performed their hasty toilet, a running fire of "chaff" and good-humored jesting, some of which consisted of personal allusions the reverse of complimentary.

Many of the boys stopped to breakfast, but not all. Some wanted to get to work earlier, and took breakfast at a later hour at some cheap restaurant, earning it before they ate it. Ben, however, had paid for his breakfast in advance, knowing that he could not get it so cheap elsewhere, and so waited to partake of it. He took his place at a long table with his companions, and found himself served with a bowl of coffee and a generous slice of bread. Sometimes, but not always, a little cold meat is supplied in addition. But even when there is bread only, the coffee warms the stomach, and so strengthens the boys for their labors outside. The breakfast was not as varied, of course, as Ben had been accustomed to at home, nor as tempting as my young readers have spread before them every morning; but it was good of its kind, and Ben ate it with unusual relish.

When he had finished his meal, he prepared to go out to work; not, however, till the superintendent, whose recollection of individual boys is surprising, considering the large number who frequent the Lodging House in the course of a year, had invited him to come again. The Lodging House, though it cannot supply the place of a private home, steps between hundreds of boys and complete vagabondage, into which, but for its existence, they would quickly lapse. Probably no money is more wisely expended than that which enables the Children's Aid Society of New York to maintain this and kindred institutions.

Ben had, after breakfast, eighty-five cents to commence the day on. But of this sum, it will be remembered, he had reserved fifty cents to pay the friendly reporter for his loan. This left him a working capital of thirty-five cents. It was not a large sum to do business on, but it was enough, and with it Ben felt quite independent.

In front of the 'Times' office, Ben met Rough and Ready,—the newsboy who had taken his part the day before. He had got the start of Ben, and was just disposing of his only remaining paper.

"How are you?" asked Ben.

"So's to be around," answered the other. "What are you up to?"

"I'm going to buy some papers."

"I have sold eight already. Where did you sleep last night?"

"At the Lodging House."

"How do you like it?"

"It's a good place, and very cheap."

"Yes, it's a bully place. I'd go there myself, if it wasn't for mother and Rose. It's enough sight better than our room on Leonard Street. But I can't leave my mother and sister."

"If you're going to buy some more papers, I'd like to go with you."

"All right. Come ahead."

Ben invested his money under the direction of his companion. By his advice, he purchased nearly to the amount of his entire capital, knowing that it would come back to him again, so that his plan for paying the reporter could still be carried out.

"You can stand near me, if you want to, Ben," said Rough and Ready.

"I am afraid I shall interfere with your trade," answered Ben.

"Don't be afraid of that. I don't ask no favors. I can get my share of business."

Ben, while engaged in selling papers himself, had an opportunity to watch the ready tact with which Rough and Ready adapted himself to the different persons whom he encountered. He succeeded in effecting a sale in many cases where others would have failed. He had sold all his papers before Ben had disposed of two-thirds of his, though both began with an equal number.

"Here, Ben," he said, generously, "give me three of your papers, I'll sell 'em for you."

By this friendly help, Ben found himself shortly empty-handed.

"Shall I buy any more?" he inquired of his companion.

"It's gettin' late for mornin' papers," said Rough and Ready. "You'd better wait till the evenin' papers come out. How much money have you made?"

Ben counted over his money, and answered, "I've made thirty-five cents."

"Well, that'll be more'n enough to buy your dinner."

"How much do you make in a day?" asked Ben.

"Sometimes over a dollar."

"You ought to lay up money, then."

Rough and Ready shook his head.

"I have to pay everything over to my mother," he said. "It's little enough to support a family."

"Doesn't your father earn anything?"

"My *step*-father," repeated the other, emphasizing the first syllable. "No, he doesn't earn much, and what he does earn, he spends for rum. We could do a great deal better without him," he continued.

Ben began to see that he had a much easier task before him in supporting himself, than his new friend in supplying the wants of a family of four; for Mr. Martin, his step-father, did not scruple to live partially on the earnings of his step-son, whose industry should have put him to shame.

"I guess I'll go home a little while," said Rough and Ready. "I'll see you again this afternoon."

Left to himself, Ben began to walk around with an entirely different feeling from that which he experienced the day before. He had one dollar and twenty cents in his pocket; not all of it his own, but the greater part of it his own earnings. Only twenty-four hours before his prospects seemed very dark. Now he had found friends, and he had also learned how to help himself.

As he was walking down Nassau Street, he suddenly espied, a little distance ahead, the reporter who had done him such an important service the day before.

He quickened his pace, and speedily came up with him.

"Good-morning," said he, by way of calling the reporter's attention.

"Good-morning," responded the reporter, not at first recognizing him.

"I'm ready to pay the money you lent me yesterday," said Ben.

"Oh, you're the boy I set up in business yesterday. Well, how have you made out?"

"Pretty well," said Ben, with satisfaction. "Here's the money you lent me;" and he drew out fifty cents, and offered it to the young man.

"But have you got any money left?" inquired the reporter.

Ben displayed the remainder of his money, mentioning the amount.

"You've succeeded capitally. Where did you sleep last night?"

"At the Newsboys' Lodge."

"That's better than sleeping out. I begin to think, my young friend, you must have a decided business talent. It isn't often a new boy succeeds so well."

Ben was pleased with this compliment, and made a new offer of the money, which the young man had not yet taken.

"I don't know as I had better take this money," said the reporter; "you may need it."

"No," said Ben, "I've got enough to keep me along."

"You've got to get dinner."

"That won't cost me more than twenty-five cents; then I shall have forty-five to buy papers this afternoon."

"Well," said the young man, "if you don't need it, I will take it; but on one condition."

"What is that?" asked Ben.

"That if you get hard up at any time, you will come to me, and I will help you out."

"Thank you," said Ben, gratefully. "You are very kind."

"I know that you boys are apt to have hard times; but if you work faithfully and don't form any bad habits, I think you will get along. Here is my card, and directions for finding me, if you need any assistance at any time."

Ben took the card, and went on his way, feeling more glad that he had paid his debt than if the money were still in his possession. He felt that it was a partial atonement for the theft which he had nearly committed the day before.

As he walked along, thinking of what he had just done, he suddenly found himself shoved violently off the sidewalk. Looking angrily to see who was the aggressor, he recognized Mike Rafferty, who had been detected the night before in wearing his stolen shirt.

"What's that for?" demanded Ben, angrily.

"It's to tache you better manners, ye spalpeen!" said Mike.

Ben returned the blow with spirit.

"That's to teach you not to steal my shirt again," he said.

"It's a lie," said Mike. "I bought it of the man you sold it to."

"You know better," retorted Ben. "You took it while I was asleep in the Park."

Mike was about to retaliate with another blow, when the sight of an approaching policeman warned him of peril, and he retreated in good order, sending back looks of defiance at our hero, whom he could not forgive for having proved him guilty of theft.

Ben's exploration of the city had thus far been very limited. He had heard of the Battery, and he determined to go down there. The distance was not great, and in a few minutes he found himself at the lower end of the Manhattan Island, looking with interest at the shores across the river. Here was Castle Garden, a large structure, now used for recently arrived emigrants, but once the scene of one of Jenny Lind's triumphs. Now it would seem very strange to have a grand concert given in such a building and in such a locality. However, Ben knew nothing of the purposes of the building, and looked at it ignorantly. The Battery he thought might once have been pretty; but now the grass has been worn off by pedestrians, and the once fashionable houses in the neighborhood have long ago been deserted by their original proprietors, and been turned into warehouses, or cheap boarding-houses.

After looking about a little, Ben turned to go back. He began to feel hungry, and thought he might as well get some dinner. After that was eaten it would be time for the evening papers. He was intending to go back to Fulton Street; but his attention was drawn to a restaurant by the bills of fare exposed outside. A brief examination satisfied him that the prices were quite as moderate as in Fulton Street, and he decided to enter, and take his dinner here.

CHAPTER XI

BEN BECOMES A BAGGAGE-SMASHER

The restaurant was a small one, and not fashionable in appearance, having a shabby look. The floor was sanded, and the tables were covered with soiled cloths. However, Ben had learned already not to be fastidious, and he sat down and gave his order. A plate of roast beef and a cup of coffee were brought, according to his directions. Seated opposite him at the table was a man who had nearly completed his dinner as Ben commenced. He held in his hand a Philadelphia paper, which he left behind when he rose to go.

"You have left your paper," said Ben.

"I have read it through," was the reply. "I don't care to take it."

Ben took it up, and found it to be a daily paper which his father had been accustomed to take for years. It gave him a start, as he saw the familiar page, and he felt a qualm of homesickness. The neat house in which he had lived since he was born, his mother's gentle face, rose up before him, compared with his present friendless condition, and the tears rose to his eyes. But he was in a public restaurant, and his pride came to the rescue. He pressed back the tears, and resumed his knife and fork.

When he had finished his dinner, he took up the paper once more, reading here and there. At last his eye rested on the following advertisement:—

"My son, Benjamin Brandon, having run away from home without any good reason, I hereby caution the public against trusting him on my account; but will pay the sum of one dollar and necessary expenses to any person who will return him to me. He is ten years old, well grown for his age, has dark eyes and a dark complexion. He was dressed in a gray-mixed suit, and had on a blue cap when he left home.

James Brandon.

Ben's face flushed when he read this advertisement. It was written by his father, he knew well enough, and he judged from the language that it was written in anger. *One dollar* was offered for his restoration.

Ben felt somehow humiliated at the smallness of the sum, and at the thought that this advertisement would be read by his friends and school-companions. The softer thoughts, which but just now came to him, were banished, and he determined, whatever hardships awaited him, to remain in New York, and support himself as he had begun to do. But, embittered as he felt against his father, he felt a pang when he thought of his mother. He knew how anxious she would feel about him, and he wished he might be able to write her privately that he was well, and doing well. But he was afraid the letter would get into his father's hands, and reveal his whereabouts; then the police might be set on his track, and he might be forced home to endure the humiliation of a severe punishment, and the jeers of his companions, who would never let him hear the last of his abortive attempt.

At last a way occurred to him. He would write a letter, and place it in the hands of someone going to Philadelphia, to be posted in the latter city. This would give no clue to his present home, and would answer the purpose of relieving his mother's anxiety.

Late in the afternoon, Ben went into a stationery store on Nassau Street.

"Will you give me a sheet of paper, and an envelope?" he asked, depositing two cents on the counter.

The articles called for were handed him.

"Can I write a letter here?" inquired Ben.

"You can go round to that desk," said the clerk; "you will find pen and ink there."

Ben, with some difficulty, composed and wrote the following letter, for it was the first he had ever had occasion to write:—

"Dear Mother,—I hope you will not feel very bad because I have left home. Father punished me for what I did not do, and after that I was not willing to stay; but I wish I could see you. Don't feel anxious about me, for I am getting along very well, and earning my own living. I cannot tell you where I am, for father might find out, and I do not want to come back, especially after that advertisement. I don't think my going will make much difference to father, as he has only offered one dollar reward for me. You need not show this letter to him. I send you my love, and I also send my love to Mary, though she used to tease me sometimes. And now I must bid you good-by.

From your affectionate son,
Ben."

After completing this letter Ben put it in the envelope, and directed it to

"Mrs. Ruth Brandon,
"Cedarville,
"Pennsylvania."

It may be explained that the Mary referred to was an elder sister, ten years older than Ben, against whom he felt somewhat aggrieved, on account of his sister's having interfered with him more than he thought she had any right to do. She and Ben were the only children.

If I were to express my opinion of this letter of Ben's, I should say that it was wanting in proper feeling for the mother who had always been kind and gentle to him, and whose heart, he must have known, would be deeply grieved by his running away from home. But Ben's besetting sin was pride, mingled with obstinacy, and pride prevailed over his love for his mother. If he could have known of the bitter tears which his mother was even now shedding over her lost boy, I think he would have found it difficult to maintain his resolution.

When the letter was written, Ben went across to the post-office, and bought a three-cent stamp, which he placed on the envelope. Then, learning that there was an evening train for Philadelphia, he went down to the Cortlandt Street Ferry, and watched till he saw a gentleman, who had the air of a traveller. Ben stepped up to him and inquired, "Are you going to Philadelphia, sir?"

"Yes, my lad," was the answer; "are you going there also?"

"No, sir."

"I thought you might want somebody to take charge of you. Is there anything I can do for you?"

"Yes, sir. If you would be so kind as to post this letter in Philadelphia."

"I will do so; but why don't you post it in New York? It will go just as well."

"The person who wrote it," said Ben, "doesn't want to have it known where it came from."

"Very well, give it to me, and I will see that it is properly mailed."

The gentleman took the letter, and Ben felt glad that it was written. He thought it would relieve his mother's anxiety.

As he was standing on the pier, a gentleman having a carpet-bag in one hand, and a bundle of books in the other, accosted him.

"Can you direct me to the Astor House, boy?"

"Yes, sir," said Ben.

Then, with a sudden thought, he added, "Shall I carry your carpet-bag, sir?"

"On the whole I think you may," said the gentleman. "Or stay, I think you may take this parcel of books."

"I can carry both, sir."

"No matter about that. I will carry the bag, and you shall be my guide."

Ben had not yet had time to get very well acquainted with the city; but the Astor House, which is situated nearly opposite the lower end of the City Hall Park, he had passed a dozen times, and knew the way to it very well. He was glad that the gentleman wished to go there, and not to one of the up-town hotels, of which he knew nothing. He went straight up Cortlandt Street to Broadway, and then turning north, soon arrived at the massive structure, which, for over thirty years, has welcomed travellers from all parts of the world.

"This is the Astor House, sir," said Ben.

"I remember it now," said the gentleman; "but it is ten years since I have been in New York, and I did not feel quite certain of finding my way. Do you live in New York?"

"Yes, sir."

"You may give me the package now. How much shall I pay you for your services?"

"Whatever you please, sir," said Ben.

"Will that answer?" and the traveller placed twenty-five cents in the hands of our young hero.

"Yes, sir," said Ben, in a tone of satisfaction. "Thank you."

The traveller entered the hotel, and Ben remained outside, congratulating himself upon his good luck.

"That's an easy way to earn twenty five cents," he thought. "It didn't take me more than fifteen minutes to come up from the ferry, and I should have to sell twenty-five papers to make so much."

This sum, added to what he had made during the day by selling papers, and including what he had on hand originally, made one dollar and thirty cents. But out of this he had spent twenty-five cents for dinner, and for his letter, including postage, five cents. Thus his expenses had been thirty cents, which, being deducted, left him just one dollar. Out of this, however, it would be necessary to buy some supper, and pay for his lodging and breakfast at the Newsboys' Home. Fifteen cents, however, would do for the first, while the regular charge for the second would be but twelve cents. Ben estimated, therefore, that he would have seventy-three cents to start on next day. He felt that this was a satisfactory state of finances, and considered whether he could not afford to spend a little more for supper. However, not feeling very hungry, he concluded not to do so.

The next morning he bought papers as usual and sold them. But it seemed considerably harder work, for the money, than carrying bundles. However, Ben foresaw that in order to become a "baggage-smasher" (for this is the technical term by which the boys and men are known, who wait around the ferries and railway depots for a chance to carry baggage, though I have preferred to use the term luggage boy), it would be necessary to know more about localities in the city than he did at present. Accordingly he devoted the intervals of time between the selling of papers, to seeking out and ascertaining the locality of the principal hotels and streets in the city.

In the course of a fortnight he had obtained a very fair knowledge of the city. He now commenced waiting at the ferries and depots, though he did not immediately give up entirely the newspaper trade. But at length he gave it up altogether, and became a "baggage-smasher," by profession, or, as he is styled in the title of this book, a luggage boy.

Thus commences a new page in his history.

CHAPTER XII

BEN'S HOME IN PHILADELPHIA

Though the story of "Ben, the Luggage Boy," professes to treat of life in the city streets, I must devote a single chapter to a very different place. I must carry the reader to Ben's home in Pennsylvania, and show what effect his running away had upon the family circle.

There was a neat two-story house standing on the principal street in Cedarville, with a pleasant lawn in front, through which, from the gate, a gravelled walk ran to the front door. Mr. Brandon, as I have already said, was a coal-dealer, and in very comfortable circumstances; so that Ben had never known what it was to want anything which he really needed. He was a man of great firmness, and at times severity, and more than once Ben had felt aggrieved by his treatment of him. Mrs. Brandon was quite different from her husband, being gentle and kind, and it was to her that Ben always went for sympathy, in any trouble or difficulty, whether at home or at school.

Mrs. Brandon was sitting at the window with her work in her hand; but it had fallen listlessly in her lap, and on her face was a look of painful preoccupation. Opposite her sat her daughter Mary, Ben's only sister, already referred to.

"Don't worry so, mother," said Mary; "you will make yourself sick."

"I cannot help it, Mary," said Mrs. Brandon. "I can't help worrying about Ben. He has been gone a week now, and Heaven knows what he has suffered. He may be dead."

"No, mother," said Mary, who had more of her father's strength than her mother's gentleness. "He is not dead, you may depend upon that."

"But he had no money, that I know of. How could he live?"

"Ben can take care of himself better than most boys of his age."

"But think of a boy of ten going out in the world by himself!"

"There are many boys of ten who have to do it, mother."

"What could the poor boy do?"

"He might suffer a little; but if he does, he will the sooner come home."

"I wish he might," said Mrs. Brandon, with a sigh. "I think your father does very wrong not to go after him."

"He wouldn't know where to go. Besides, he has advertised."

"I hope Ben will not see the advertisement. Poor boy! he would feel hurt to think that we cared so little for him as to offer only one dollar for his return."

"He will know you had nothing to do with the advertisement, mother; you may be sure of that."

"Yes, he knows me too well for that. I would give all I have to have him back."

"I want him back too," said Mary. "He is my only brother, and of course I love him; but I don't think it will do him any harm to suffer a little as a punishment for going away."

"You were always hard upon the poor boy, Mary," said Mrs. Brandon.

"No, I am not hard; but I see his faults, and I want him to correct them. It is you who have been too indulgent."

"If I have been, it is because you and your father have been too much the other way."

There was a brief pause, then Mrs. Brandon said, "Can you think of any place, Mary, where Ben would be likely to go?"

"Yes, I suppose he went to Philadelphia. When a boy runs away from home, he naturally goes to the nearest city."

"I have a great mind to go up to-morrow."

"What good would it do, mother?"

"I might meet him in the street."

"There is not much chance of that. I shouldn't wonder if by this time he had gone to sea."

"Gone to sea!" repeated Mrs. Brandon, turning pale. "What makes you think so? Did he ever speak of such a thing to you?"

"Yes, he once threatened to run away to sea, when I did something that did not suit him."

"Oh, I hope not. I have heard that boys are treated very badly on board ship. Besides, he might get drowned."

"I am not sure whether a good sea-voyage might not be the best thing for him," said strong-minded Mary.

"But suppose he should be ill-treated?"

"It might take the pride out of him, and make him a better boy."

"I never get much satisfaction from you, Mary. I don't see how you can be so harsh."

"I see we are not likely to agree, mother. But there is a boy coming up the walk with a letter in his hand."

"It may be from Ben," said his mother, rising hastily, and going to the door.

The boy was William Gordon, a school-mate of Ben's, whose disappearance, long before this time, had been reported throughout the village.

"I was passing the post-office, Mrs. Brandon," he said, "when the postmaster called from the window, and asked me to bring you this letter. I think it is from Ben. The handwriting looks like his."

"Oh, thank you, William," said Mrs. Brandon, joyfully. "Give it to me quick."

She tore it open and read the letter, which is given at length in the last chapter.

"Is it from Ben?" asked William.

"Yes."

"Is he in Philadelphia? I noticed it was mailed there."

"Yes—no—he says he cannot tell us where he is."

"I think he must be in Philadelphia, or the letter would not be mailed there."

"Come in, William. I must go and tell Mary."

"No, thank you, Mrs. Brandon. I am on an errand for my mother. I hope Ben is well?"

"Yes, he says so."

Mrs. Brandon went in, and showed the letter to her daughter.

"There, I told you, mother, you need not be alarmed. He says he is earning his living."

"But it seems so hard for a boy of ten to have to work for his living. What can he do?"

"Oh, there are various things he can do. He might sell papers, for instance."

"I think I shall go to Philadelphia to-morrow, Mary."

"It won't be of any use, you may depend, mother. He is not in Philadelphia."

"But this letter is posted there."

"That is a proof to me that he is not there. He says he don't want to come back."

Shortly after, Mr. Brandon entered the house.

"We have had a letter from Ben, father," said Mary.

"Show it to me," he said, briefly.

He read the letter, and handed it back without a word.

"What are you going to do about it, Mr. Brandon?" asked his wife.

"What is there to be done?" he asked.

"I think I had better go up to Philadelphia to-morrow."

"What for?"

"I might see him."

"You would be going on a wild-goose chase."

"Then why won't you go?"

"It isn't worthwhile. If the boy doesn't want to come home, he may take care of himself if he likes it so well. I shan't run round after him."

"He says he did not do what you punished him for," said Mrs. Brandon, rather deprecatingly, for she was somewhat in awe of her husband.

"Of course he would say that. I have heard that before."

"But I don't think he really did."

"I know you have always been foolishly indulgent to him."

"At any rate that cannot be said of you," said his wife, with some spirit.

"No," he answered, rather surprised at such an unusual manifestation from his usually acquiescent wife; "you are right there, and you might add that I don't mean to be, if he should return."

"I think he would have come home but for that advertisement. You see what he says about it in his letter."

"If I were to write it again, I should write it in the same manner, though perhaps I might not offer so large a sum."

Mrs. Brandon sighed, and ceased speaking. She knew her husband well enough to see that there was little chance of changing his determination, or softening his anger towards Ben.

The next day, when Mr. Brandon returned home to dinner from his coal-wharf, he found Mary seated at the head of the table.

"Where is your mother?" he asked.

"She went to Philadelphia by the middle train," was the answer.

"She has gone on a fool's errand."

"I advised her not to go; but she thought she might meet Ben, and I could not dissuade her."

"Well, she will be better satisfied after she has been up—and failed to find him."

"Do you think he will ever come back, father?"

"Yes; he will turn up again someday, like a bad penny. He will find that earning his own living is not quite so agreeable as being taken care of at home."

"Suppose he shouldn't come back?"

"So much the worse for him," said Mr. Brandon.

Mr. Brandon spoke after his way of speaking, for he was not an affectionate man, nor given to the softer emotions. He had never given Ben any reason to think he loved him, at least since he was a baby, but appearances are sometimes deceptive, and he thought more of his son's absence than anyone would have supposed. He thought, too, of that sentence in Ben's letter, in which he spoke of being punished for what he did not do, and he admitted to himself, though he would not have done so to his wife, that perhaps he had been unjust to the boy after all. Every day when he turned from his office to go home, it was with the unacknowledged hope that he might find the prodigal returned. But in this hope they were all doomed to be disappointed. Year after year passed away, and still no tidings from Ben beyond that single letter which we have mentioned.

Mrs. Brandon returned from Philadelphia, as might have been anticipated, disappointed and despondent. She was very tired, for she had wandered about the streets, looking everywhere, during the four or five hours she was in the city. Once or twice her heart beat high, as she saw in front of her a boy of Ben's size, and dressed as he had been dressed when he left home. But when, with hurrying steps she came up with him, she was doomed, in every case, to disappointment.

"I told you it would be no use, mother," said Mary.

"I couldn't stay at home contented, if I did nothing to find him, Mary."

"He'll turn up yet some day, mother,—return in rags most likely."

"Come when he may, or how he may, Mary, my arms shall be open to receive him."

But the years passed, and Ben did not come.

CHAPTER XIII

THE FIRST CIGAR

It was a week or more after Ben started in business as a bag-gage-smasher, that, in returning from carrying a carpet-bag to Lovejoy's Hotel, on Broadway, he fell in with his first city acquaintance, Jerry Collins. Jerry had just "polished up" a gentleman's boots, and, having been unusually lucky this morning in securing shines, felt disposed to be lavish.

"How are you, Ben?" asked Jerry. "What are you up to now?"

"I'm a baggage-smasher," answered Ben, who was beginning to adopt the language of the streets.

"How does it pay?"

"Well," said Ben, "sometimes it pays first rate, when I'm lucky. Other days I don't get much to do. I didn't make but fifteen cents this morning. I carried a bag up to Lovejoy's, and that's all the man would pay me."

"I've made fifty cents this mornin'. Look here, Johnny."

The Johnny addressed was a boy who sold cigars, four for ten cents.

"I'll take two," said Jerry, producing five cents.

"Six cents for two," said the cigar boy.

"All right, I'll owe you the other cent," said Jerry, coolly.

"Do you smoke?" inquired Ben.

"In course I do. Don't you?"

"No."

"Why don't you?"

"I don't know," said Ben. "Do you like it?"

"It's bully. Here, take this cigar. I bought it for you."

Ben hesitated; but finally, induced mainly by a curiosity to see how it seemed, accepted the cigar, and lighted it by Jerry's. The two boys sat down on an empty box, and Jerry instructed Ben how to puff. Ben did not particularly enjoy it; but thought he might as well learn now as any other time. His companion puffed away like a veteran smoker; but after a while Ben's head began to swim, and he felt sick at his stomach.

"I don't feel well," he said. "I guess I'll stop smoking."

"Oh, go ahead," said Jerry. "It's only because it's the first time. You'll like it after a while."

Thus encouraged, Ben continued to smoke, though his head and his stomach got continually worse.

"I don't like it," gasped Ben, throwing down the cigar. "I'm going to stop."

"You've got a healthy color," said Jerry, slyly.

"I'm afraid I'm going to be awful sick," said Ben, whose sensations were very far from comfortable. Just at this moment, ignorant of the brief character of his present feelings, he heartily wished himself at home, for the first time since his arrival in the city.

"You do look rather green," said Jerry. "Maybe you're going to have the cholera. I've heard that there's some cases round."

This suggestion alarmed Ben, who laid his head down between his knees, and began to feel worse than ever.

"Don't be scared," said Jerry, thinking it time to relieve Ben's mind. "It's only the cigar. You'll feel all right in a jiffy."

While Ben was experiencing the disagreeable effects of his first cigar, he resolved never to smoke another. But, as might have been expected, he felt differently on recovering. It was not long before he could puff away with as much enjoyment and unconcern as any of his street companions, and a part of his earnings were consumed in this way. It may be remarked here that the street boy does not always indulge in the luxury of a whole cigar. Sometimes he picks up a fragment which has been discarded by the original smoker. There are some small dealers, who make it a business to collect these "stubs," or employ others to do so, and then sell them to the street boys, at a penny apiece, or less, according to size. Sometimes these stubs are bought in preference to a cheap cigar, because they are apt to be of a superior quality. Ben, however, never smoked "stubs." In course of time he became very much like other street boys; but in some respects his taste was more fastidious, and he preferred to indulge himself in a cheap cigar, which was not second-hand.

We must now pass rapidly over the six years which elapsed from the date of Ben's first being set adrift in the streets to the period at which our story properly begins. These years have been fruitful of change to our young adventurer. They have changed him from a country boy of ten, to a self-reliant and independent street boy of sixteen. The impressions left by his early and careful home-training have been mostly effaced. Nothing in his garb now distinguishes him from the class of which he is a type. He has long since ceased to care for neat or whole attire, or carefully brushed hair. His straggling locks, usually long, protrude from an aperture in his hat. His shoes would make a very poor advertisement for the shoemaker by whom they were originally manufactured. His face is not always free from stains, and his street companions have long since ceased to charge him with putting on airs, on account of the superior neatness of his personal appearance. Indeed, he has become rather a favorite among them, in consequence of his frankness, and his willingness at all times to lend a helping hand to a comrade temporarily "hard up." He has adopted to a great extent the tastes and habits of the class to which he belongs, and bears with acquired philosophy the hardships and privations which fall to their lot. Like "Ragged Dick," he has a sense of humor, which is apt to reveal itself in grotesque phrases, or amusing exaggerations.

Of course his education, so far as education is obtained from books, has not advanced at all. He has not forgotten how to read, having occasion to read the daily papers. Occasionally, too, he indulges himself in a dime novel, the more sensational the better, and is sometimes induced to read therefrom to a group of companions whose attainments are even less than his own.

It may be asked whether he ever thinks of his Pennsylvania home, of his parents and his sister. At first he thought of them frequently; but by degrees he became so accustomed to the freedom and independence of his street life, with its constant variety, that he would have been unwilling to return, even if the original cause of his leaving home were removed. Life in a Pennsylvania village seemed "slow" compared with the excitement of his present life.

In the winter, when the weather was inclement, and the lodging accommodations afforded by the street were not particularly satisfactory, Ben found it convenient to avail himself of the cheap lodgings furnished by the Newsboys' Lodging House; but at other times, particularly in the warm summer nights, he saved his six cents, and found a lodging for himself among the wharves, or in some lane or alley. Of the future he did not think much. Like street boys in general, his horizon was limited by the present. Sometimes, indeed, it did occur to him that he could not be a luggage boy all his lifetime. Some time or other he must take up something else. However, Ben carelessly concluded that he could make a living somehow or other, and as to old age that was too far ahead to disquiet himself about.

CHAPTER XIV

THE PASSENGER FROM ALBANY

Ben did not confine himself to any particular pier or railway depot, but stationed himself now at one, now at another, according as the whim seized him, or as the prospect of profit appeared more or less promising. One afternoon he made his way to the pier at which the Albany boats landed. He knew the hour of arrival, not only for the river-boats, but for most of the inward trains, for this was required by his business.

He had just finished smoking a cheap cigar when the boat arrived. The passengers poured out, and the usual bustle ensued. Now was the time for Ben to be on the alert. He scanned the outcoming passengers with an attentive eye, fixing his attention upon those who were encumbered with carpet-bags, valises, or bundles. These he marked out as his possible patrons, and accosted them professionally.

"Smash yer baggage, sir?" he said to a gentleman carrying a valise.

The latter stared hard at Ben, evidently misunderstanding him, and answered irascibly, "Confound your impudence, boy; what do you mean?"

"Smash yer baggage, sir?"

"If you smash my baggage, I'll smash your head."

"Thank you, sir, for your kind offer; but my head aint insured," said Ben, who saw the joke, and enjoyed it.

"Look here, boy," said the puzzled traveller, "what possible good would it do you to smash my baggage?"

"That's the way I make a livin'," said Ben.

"Do you mean to say any persons are foolish enough to pay you for destroying their baggage? You must be crazy, or else you must think I am."

"Not destroying it, smashin' it."

"What's the difference?"

Here a person who had listened to the conversation with some amusement interposed.

"If you will allow me to explain, sir, the boy only proposes to carry your valise. He is what we call a 'baggage-smasher,' and carrying it is called 'smashing.'"

"Indeed, that's a very singular expression to use. Well, my lad, I think I understand you now. You have no hostile intentions, then?"

"Nary a one," answered Ben.

"Then I may see fit to employ you. Of course you know the way everywhere?"

"Yes, sir."

"You may take my valise as far as Broadway. There I shall take a stage."

Ben took the valise, and raising it to his shoulders was about to precede his patron.

"You can walk along by my side," said the gentleman; "I want to talk to you."

"All right, governor," said Ben. "I'm ready for an interview."

"How do you like 'baggage-smashing,' as you call it?"

"I like it pretty well when I'm workin' for a liberal gentleman like you," said Ben, shrewdly.

"What makes you think I am liberal?" asked the gentleman, smiling.

"I can tell by your face," answered our hero.

"But you get disappointed sometimes, don't you?"

"Yes, sometimes," Ben admitted.

"Tell me some of your experiences that way."

"Last week," said Ben, "I carried a bag, and a thunderin' heavy one, from the Norwich boat to French's Hotel,—a mile and a half I guess it was,—and how much do you think the man paid me?"

"Twenty-five cents."

"Yes, he did, but he didn't want to. All he offered me first was ten cents."

"That's rather poor pay. I don't think I should want to work for that myself."

"You couldn't live very high on such pay," said Ben.

"I have worked as cheap, though."

"You have!" said Ben, surprised.

"Yes, my lad, I was a poor boy once,—as poor as you are."

"Where did you live?" asked Ben, interested.

"In a country town in New England. My father died early, and I was left alone in the world. So I hired myself out to a farmer for a dollar a week and board. I had to be up at five every morning, and work all day. My wages, you see, amounted to only about sixteen cents a day and board for twelve hours' work."

"Why didn't you run away?" inquired Ben.

"I didn't know where to run to."

"I s'pose you aint workin' for that now?" said our hero.

"No, I've been promoted," said the gentleman, smiling. "Of course I got higher pay, as I grew older. Still, at twenty-one I found myself with only two hundred dollars. I worked a year longer till it became three hundred, and then I went out West,—to Ohio,—where I took up a quarter-section of land, and became a farmer on my own account. Since then I've dipped into several things, have bought more land, which has increased in value on my hands, till now I am probably worth fifty thousand dollars."

"I'm glad of it," said Ben.

"Why?"

"Because you can afford to pay me liberal for smashin' your baggage."

"What do you call liberal?" inquired his patron, smiling.

"Fifty cents," answered Ben, promptly.

"Then I will be liberal. Now, suppose you tell me something about yourself. How long have you been a 'baggage-smasher,' as you call it?"

"Six years," said Ben.

"You must have begun young. How old are you now?"

"Sixteen."

"You'll soon be a man. What do you intend to do then?"

"I haven't thought much about it," said Ben, with truth.

"You don't mean to carry baggage all your life, do you?"

"I guess not," answered Ben. "When I get to be old and infirm, I'm goin' into some light, genteel employment, such as keepin' a street stand."

"So that is your highest ambition, is it?" asked the stranger.

"I don't think I've got any ambition," said Ben. "As long as I make a livin', I don't mind."

"When you see well-dressed gentlemen walking down Broadway, or riding in their carriages, don't you sometimes think it would be agreeable if you could be in their place?"

"I should like to have a lot of money," said Ben. "I wouldn't mind bein' the president of a bank, or a railway-director, or somethin' of that kind."

"I am afraid you have never thought seriously upon the subject of your future," said Ben's companion, "or you wouldn't be satisfied with your present business."

"What else can I do? I'd rather smash baggage than sell papers or black boots."

"I would not advise either. I'll tell you what you ought to do, my young friend. You should leave the city, and come out West. I'll give you something to do on one of my farms, and promote you as you are fit for it."

"You're very kind," said Ben, more seriously; "but I shouldn't like it."

"Why not?"

"I don't want to leave the city. Here there's somethin' goin' on. I'd miss the streets and the crowds. I'd get awful lonesome in the country."

"Isn't it better to have a good home in the country than to live as you do in the city?"

"I like it well enough," said Ben. "We're a jolly crowd, and we do as we please. There aint nobody to order us round 'cept the copps, and they let us alone unless we steal, or something of that kind."

"So you are wedded to your city life?"

"Yes, I guess so; though I don't remember when the weddin' took place."

"And you prefer to live on in your old way?"

"Yes, sir; thank you all the same."

"You may change your mind some time, my lad. If you ever do, and will write to me at B——, Ohio, I will send for you to come out. Here is my card."

"Thank you, sir," said Ben. "I'll keep the card, and if ever I change my mind, I'll let you know."

They had been walking slowly, or they would have reached Broadway sooner. They had now arrived there, and the stranger bade Ben good-by, handing him at the same time the fifty cents agreed upon.

"He's a brick," Ben soliloquized, "even if he did say he'd smash my head. I hope I'll meet some more like him."

Ben's objection to leaving the city is felt in an equal degree by many boys who are situated like himself. Street life has its privations and actual sufferings; but for all that there is a wild independence and freedom from restraint about it, which suits those who follow it. To be at the beck and call of no one; to be responsible only to themselves, provided they keep from violating the law, has a charm to these young outcasts. Then, again, they become accustomed to the street and its varied scenes, and the daily excitement of life in a large city becomes such a matter of necessity to them, that they find the country lonesome. Yet, under the auspices of the Children's Aid Society, companies of boys are continually being sent out to the great West with the happiest results. After a while the first loneliness wears away, and they become interested in the new scenes and labors to which they are introduced, and a large number have already grown up to hold respectable, and, in some cases, prominent places, in the communities which they have joined. Others have pined for the city, until they could no longer resist their yearning for it, and have found their way back to the old, familiar scenes, to resume the former life of suffering and privation. Such is the strange fascination which their lawless and irresponsible mode of life oftentimes exerts upon the minds of these young Arabs of the street.

When Ben parted from the passenger by the Albany boat, he did not immediately seek another job. Accustomed as he was to live from "hand to mouth," he had never troubled himself much about accumulating more than would answer his immediate needs. Some boys in the Lodging House made deposits in the bank of that institution; but frugality was not one of Ben's virtues. As long as he came out even at the end of the day, he felt very well satisfied. Generally he went penniless to bed; his business not being one that required him to reserve money for capital to carry it on. In the case of a newsboy it was different. He must keep enough on hand to buy a supply of papers in the morning, even if he were compelled to go to bed supperless.

With fifty cents in his pocket, Ben felt rich. It would buy him a good supper, besides paying for his lodging at the Newsboys' Home, and a ticket for the Old Bowery besides,—that is, a fifteen-cent ticket, which, according to the arrangement of that day, would admit him to one of the best-located seats in the house, that is, in the pit, corresponding to what is known as the parquette in other theatres. This arrangement has now been changed, so that the street boys find themselves banished to the upper gallery of their favorite theatre. But in the days of which I am speaking they made themselves conspicuous in the front rows, and were by no means bashful in indicating their approbation or disapprobation of the different actors who appeared on the boards before them.

Ben had not gone far when he fell in with an acquaintance,—Barney Flynn.

"Where you goin', Ben?" inquired Barney.

"Goin' to get some grub," answered Ben.

"I'm with you, then. I haven't eat anything since mornin', and I'm awful hungry."

"Have you got any stamps?"

"I've got a fifty."

"So have I."

"Where are you goin' for supper?"

"To Pat's, I guess."

"All right; I'll go with you."

The establishment known as "Pat's" is located in a basement in Nassau Street, as the reader of "Mark, the Match Boy," will remember. It is, of coarse, a cheap restaurant, and is considerably frequented by the street boys, who here find themselves more welcome guests than at some of the more pretentious eating-houses.

Ben and Barney entered, and gave their orders for a substantial repast. The style in which the meal was served differed considerably from the service at Delmonico's; but it is doubtful whether any of the guests at the famous up-town restaurant enjoyed their meal any better than the two street boys, each of whom was blest with a "healthy" appetite. Barney had eaten nothing since morning, and Ben's fast had only been broken by the eating of a two-cent apple, which had not been sufficient to satisfy his hunger.

Notwithstanding the liberality of their orders, however, each of the boys found himself, at the end of the meal, the possessor of twenty-five cents. This was not a very large sum to sleep on, but it was long since either had waked up in the morning with so large a capital to commence operations upon.

"What shall we do?" asked Ben.

"Suppose we go to the Old Bowery," suggested Barney.

"Or Tony Pastor's," amended Ben.

"I like the Bowery best. There's a great fight, and a feller gets killed on the stage. It's a stunnin' old play."

"Then let us go," said Ben, who, as well as his companion, liked the idea of witnessing a stage fight, which was all the more attractive on account of having a fatal termination.

As the theatre tickets would cost but fifteen cents each, the boys felt justified in purchasing each a cheap cigar, which they smoked as they walked leisurely up Chatham Street.

CHAPTER XV

THE ROOM UNDER THE WHARF

It was at a late hour when the boys left the theatre. The play had been of a highly sensational character, and had been greeted with enthusiastic applause on the part of the audience, particularly the occupants of the "pit." Now, as they emerged from the portals of the theatre, various characteristic remarks of a commendatory character were interchanged.

"How'd you like it, Ben?" asked Barney.

"Bully," said Ben.

"I liked the fight best," said Barney. "Jones give it to him just about right."

"Yes, that was good," said Ben; "but I liked it best where Alphonso says to Montmorency, 'Caitiff, beware, or, by the heavens above, my trusty sword shall drink thy foul heart's blood!'"

Ben gave this with the stage emphasis, so far as he could imitate it. Barney listened admiringly.

"I say, Ben," he replied, "you did that bully. You'd make a tip-top actor."

"Would I?" said Ben, complacently. "I think I'd like to try it if I knew enough. How much money have you got, Barney?"

"Nary a red. I spent the last on peanuts."

"Just my case. We'll have to find some place to turn in for the night."

"I know a place," said Barney, "if they'll let us in."

"Whereabouts is it?"

"Down to Dover Street wharf."

"What sort of a place is it? There aint any boxes or old wagons, are there?"

"No, it's under the wharf,—a bully place."

"Under the wharf! It's wet, isn't it?"

"No, you just come along. I'll show you."

Having no other place to suggest, Ben accepted his companion's guidance, and the two made their way by the shortest route to the wharf named. It is situated not far from Fulton Ferry on the east side. It may be called a double wharf. As originally built, it was found too low for the class of vessels that used it, and another flooring was built over the first, leaving a considerable space between the two. Its capabilities for a private rendezvous occurred to a few boys, who forthwith proceeded to avail themselves of it. It was necessary to carry on their proceedings secretly; otherwise there was danger of interference from the city police. What steps they took to make their quarters comfortable will shortly be described.

When they reached the wharf, Barney looked about him with an air of caution, which Ben observed.

"What are you scared of?" asked Ben.

"We mustn't let the 'copp' see us," said Barney, "Don't make no noise."

Thus admonished, Ben followed his companion with as little noise as possible.

"How do you get down there?" he asked.

"I'll show you," said Barney.

He went to the end of the wharf, and, motioning Ben to look over, showed him a kind of ladder formed by nailing strips of wood, at regular intervals, from the outer edge down to the water's edge. This was not an arrangement of the boys, but was for the accommodation of river-boats landing at the wharf.

"I'll go down first," whispered Barney. "If the 'copp' comes along, move off, so he won't notice nothin'."

"All right!" said Ben.

Barney got part way down the ladder, when a head was protruded from below, and a voice demanded, "Who's there?"

"It's I,—Barney Flynn."

"Come along, then."

"I've got a fellow with me," continued Barney.

"Who is it?"

"It's Ben, the baggage-smasher. He wants to stop here to-night."

"All right; we can trust him."

"Come along, Ben," Barney called up the ladder.

Ben quickly commenced the descent. Barney was waiting for him, and held out his hand to help him off. Our hero stepped from the ladder upon the lower flooring of the wharf, and looked about him with some curiosity. It was certainly a singular spectacle that met his view. About a dozen boys were congregated in the room under the wharf, and had evidently taken some pains to make themselves comfortable. A carpet of good size was spread over a portion of the flooring. Upon this three beds were spread, each occupied by three boys. Those who could not be accommodated in this way laid on the carpet. Some of the boys were already asleep; two were smoking, and conversing in a low voice. Looking about him Ben recognized acquaintances in several of them.[1]

"Is that you, Mike Sweeny?" he asked of a boy stretched out on the nearest bed.

"Yes," said Mike; "come and lay alongside of me."

There was no room on the bed, but Ben found space beside it on the carpet, and accordingly stretched himself out.

"How do you like it?" asked Mike.

"Tip-top," said Ben. "How'd you get the carpet and beds? Did you buy 'em?"

"Yes," said Mike, with a wink; "but the man wasn't in, and we didn't pay for 'em."

"You stole them, then?"

"We took 'em," said Mike, who had an objection to the word stole.

"How did you get them down here without the copp seein' you?"

"We hid 'em away in the daytime, and didn't bring 'em here till night. We came near gettin' caught."

"How long have you been down here?"

"Most a month."

"It's a good place."

"Yes," said Mike, "and the rent is very reasonable. We don't have to pay nothin' for lodgin'. It's cheaper'n the Lodge."

"That's so," said Ben. "I'm sleepy," he said, gaping. "I've been to the Old Bowery to-night. Good-night!"

"Good-night!"

In five minutes Ben was fast asleep. Half an hour later, and not a sound was heard in the room under the wharf except the occasional deep breathing of some of the boys. The policeman who trod his beat nearby little suspected that just at hand, and almost under his feet, was a rendezvous of street vagrants and juvenile thieves, for such I am sorry to say was the character of some of the boys who frequented these cheap lodgings.

---

[1] The description of the room under the wharf, and the circumstances of its occupation by a company of street boys, are not imaginary. It was finally discovered, and broken up by the police, the details being given, at the time, in the daily papers, as some of my New York readers will remember. Discovery did not take place, however, until it had been occupied some time.

In addition to the articles already described there were two or three chairs, which had been contributed by different members of the organization.

Ben slept soundly through the night. When he woke up, the gray morning light entering from the open front towards the sea had already lighted up indistinctly the space between the floors. Two or three of the boys were already sitting up, yawning and stretching themselves after their night's slumber. Among these was Mike Sweeny.

"Are you awake, Ben?" he asked.

"Yes," said Ben; "I didn't hardly know where I was at first."

"It's a bully place, isn't it?"

"That's so. How'd you come across it?"

"Oh, some of us boys found it out. We've been sleepin' here a month."

"Won't you let a feller in?"

"We might let you in. I'll speak to the boys."

"I'd like to sleep here," said Ben. "It's a good deal better than sleepin' out round. Who runs the hotel?"

"Well, I'm one of 'em."

"You might call it Swceny's Hotel," suggested Ben, laughing.

"I aint the boss; Jim Bagley's got most to do with it."

"Which is he?"

"That's he, over on the next bed."

"What does he do?"

"He's a travellin' match merchant."

"That sounds big."

"Jim's smart,—he is. He makes more money'n any of us."

"Where does he travel?"

"Once he went to Californy in the steamer. He got a steerage ticket for seventy-five dollars; but he made more'n that blackin' boots for the other passengers afore they got there. He stayed there three months, and then came home."

"Does he travel now?"

"Yes, he buys a lot of matches, and goes up the river or down into Jersey, and is gone a week. A little while ago he went to Buffalo."

"Oh, yes; I know where that is."

"Blest if I do."

"It's in the western part of York State, just across from Canada."

"Who told you?"

"I learned it in school."

"I didn't know you was a scholar, Ben."

"I aint now. I've forgot most all I ever knew. I haven't been to school since I was ten years old."

"Where was that?"

"In the country."

"Well, I never went to school more'n a few weeks. I can read a little, but not much."

"It costs a good deal to go to Buffalo. How did Jim make it while he was gone?"

"Oh, he came home with ten dollars in his pocket besides payin' his expenses."

"What does Jim do with all his money?"

"He's got a mother and sister up in Bleecker Street, or some-wheres round there. He pays his mother five dollars a week, be-sides takin' care of himself."

"Why don't he live with his mother?"

"He'd rather be round with the boys."

I may remark here that Jim Bagley is a real character, and all that has been said about him is derived from information given by himself, in a conversation held with him at the Newsboys' Lodg-ing House. He figures here, however, under an assumed name, partly because the record in which his real name is preserved has been mislaid. The impression made upon the mind of the writer was, that Jim had unusual business ability and self-reliance, and might possibly develop into a successful and prosperous man of business.

Jim by this time was awake.

"Jim Bagley," said Mike, "here's a feller would like to put up at our hotel."

"Who is he?" asked Jim.

The travelling match merchant, as Mike had described him, was a boy of fifteen, rather small of his age, with a keen black eye, and a quick, decided, business-like way.

"It's this feller,—he's a baggage-smasher," explained Mike.

"All right," said Jim; "he can come if he'll pay his share."

"How much is it?" asked Ben.

Mike explained that it was expected of each guest to bring some-thing that would add to the comforts of the rendezvous. Two boys had contributed the carpet, for which probably they had paid nothing; Jim had supplied a bed, for which he did pay, as "tak-ing things without leave" was not in his line. Three boys had each contributed a chair. Thus all the articles which had been accu-mulated were individual contributions. Ben promised to pay his admission fee in the same way, but expressed a doubt whether he might not have to wait a few days, in order to save money enough to make a purchase. He never stole himself, though his association with street boys, whose principles are not always very strict on this point, had accustomed him to regard theft as a venial fault, provided it was not found out. For his own part, however, he did not care to run the risk of detection. Though he had cut himself off from his old home, he still felt that he should not like to have the report reach home that he had been convicted of dishonesty.

At an early hour the boys shook off their slumbers, and one by one left the wharf to enter upon their daily work. The newsboys were the first to go, as they must be on hand at the newspaper offices early to get their supply of papers, and fold them in readiness for early customers. The boot-blacks soon followed, as most of them were under the necessity of earning their breakfast before they ate it. Ben also got up early, and made his way to the pier of the Stonington line of steamers from Boston. These usually arrived at an early hour, and there was a good chance of a job in Ben's line when the passengers landed.

CHAPTER XVI

BEN MEETS AN OLD FRIEND

Ben had about half an hour to wait for the arrival of the steamer. Among the passengers who crossed the plank from the steamer to the pier was a gentleman of middle age, and a boy about a year younger than Ben. The boy had a carpet-bag in his hand; the father, for such appeared to be the relationship, carried a heavy valise, besides a small bundle.

"Want your baggage carried?" asked Ben, varying his usual address.

The gentleman hesitated a moment.

"You'd better let him take it, father," said the boy.

"Very well, you may take this;" and the valise was passed over to Ben.

"Give me the bag too," said Ben, addressing the boy.

"No, I'll take that. You'll have all you want to do, in carrying the valise."

They crossed the street, and here the gentleman stood still, evidently undecided about something.

"What are you thinking about, father?"

"I was thinking," the gentleman said, after a slight pause, "what I had better do."

"About what?"

"I have two or three errands in the lower part of the city, which, as my time is limited, I should like to attend to at once."

"You had better do it, then."

"What I was thinking was, that it would not be worthwhile for you to go round with me, carrying the baggage."

"Couldn't I go right up to Cousin Mary's?" asked his son.

"I am afraid you might lose the way."

"This boy will go with me. I suppose he knows the way all about the city. Don't you?" he asked, turning to Ben.

"Where do you want to go?" asked Ben.

"To No.—Madison Avenue."

"Yes, I can show you the way there well enough, but it's a good way off."

"You can both take the cars or stage when you get up to the Astor House."

"How will that do?" asked Charles, for this was his name.

"I think that will be the best plan. This boy can go with you, and you can settle with him for his services. Have you got money enough?"

"Yes, plenty."

"I will leave you here, then."

Left to themselves, it was natural that the two boys should grow social. So far as clothing went, there was certainly a wide difference between them. Ben was attired as described in the first chapter. Charles, on the other hand, wore a short sack of dark cloth, a white vest, and gray pants. A gold chain, depending from his watch-pocket, showed that he was the possessor of a watch. His whole appearance was marked by neatness and good taste. But, leaving out this difference, a keen observer might detect a considerable resemblance in the features of the two boys. Both had dark hair, black eyes, and the contour of the face was the same. I regret to add, however, that Ben's face was not so clean as it ought to have been. Among the articles contributed by the boys who lived in the room under the wharf, a washstand had not been considered necessary, and it had been long since Ben had regarded washing the face and hands as the first preparation for the labors of the day.

Charles Marston looked at his companion with some interest and curiosity. He had never lived in New York, and there was a freshness and novelty about life in the metropolis that was attractive to him.

"Is this your business?" he asked.

"What,—smashin' baggage?" inquired Ben.

"Is that what you call it?"

"Yes."

"Well, is that what you do for a living?"

"Yes," said Ben. "It's my profession, when I aint attendin' to my duties as a member of the Common Council."

"So you're a member of the city government?" asked Charles, amused.

"Yes."

"Do you have much to do that way?"

"I'm one of the Committee on Wharves," said Ben. "It's my business to see that they're right side up with care; likewise that nobody runs away with them in the night."

"How do you get paid?"

"Well, I earn my lodgin' that way just now," said Ben.

"Have you always been in this business?"

"No. Sometimes I've sold papers."

"How did you like that?"

"I like baggage-smashin' best, when I get enough to do. You don't live in the city, do you?"

"No, I live just out of Boston,—a few miles."

"Ever been in New York before?"

"Once. That was four years ago. I passed through on the way from Pennsylvania, where I used to live."

"Pennsylvania," repeated Ben, beginning to be interested. "Whereabouts did you live there,—in Philadelphy?"

"No, a little way from there, in a small town named Cedarville."

Ben started, and he nearly let fall the valise from his hand.

"What's the matter?" asked Charles.

"I came near fallin'," said Ben, a little confused. "What's your name?" he asked, rather abruptly.

"Charles Marston."

Ben scanned intently the face of his companion. He had good reason to do so, for though Charles little suspected that there was any relationship between himself and the ragged and dirty boy who carried his valise, the two were own cousins. They had been school-mates in Cedarville, and passed many a merry hour together in boyish sport. In fact Charles had been Ben's favorite playmate, as well as cousin, and many a time, when he lay awake in such chance lodgings as the street provided, he had thought of his cousin, and wished that he might meet him again. Now they had met most strangely; no longer on terms of equality, but one with all the outward appearance of a young gentleman, the other, a ragged and ignorant street boy. Ben's heart throbbed painfully when he saw that his cousin regarded him as a stranger, and for the first time in a long while he felt ashamed of his position. He would not for the world have revealed himself to Charles in his present situation; yet he felt a strong desire to learn whether he was still remembered. How to effect this without betraying his identity he hardly knew; at length he thought of a way that might lead to it.

"My name's shorter'n yours," he said.

"What is it?" asked Charles.

"It's Ben."

"That stands for Benjamin; so yours is the longest after all."

"That's so, I never thought of that. Everybody calls me Ben."

"What's your other name?"

Ben hesitated. If he said "Brandon" he would be discovered, and his pride stood in the way of that. Finally he determined to give a false name; so he answered after a slight pause, which Charles did not notice, "My other name is Hooper,—Ben Hooper. Didn't you ever know anybody of my name?"

"What,—Ben Hooper?"

"No, Ben."

"Yes. I had a cousin named Ben."

"Is he as old as you?" asked Ben, striving to speak carelessly.

"He is older if he is living; but I don't think he is living."

"Why, don't you know?"

"He ran away from home when he was ten years old, and we have never seen him since."

"Didn't he write where he had gone?"

"He wrote one letter to his mother, but he didn't say where he was. That is the last any of us heard from him."

"What sort of a chap was he?" inquired Ben. "He was a bad un, wasn't he?"

"No, Ben wasn't a bad boy. He had a quick temper though; but whenever he was angry he soon got over it."

"What made him run away from home?"

"His father punished him for something he didn't do. He found it out afterwards; but he is a stern man, and he never says anything about him. But I guess he feels bad sometimes. Father says he has grown old very fast since my cousin ran away."

"Is his mother living,—your aunt?" Ben inquired, drawn on by an impulse he could not resist.

"Yes, but she is always sad; she has never stopped mourning for Ben."

"Did you like your cousin?" Ben asked, looking wistfully in the face of his companion.

"Yes, he was my favorite cousin. Poor Ben and I were always together. I wish I knew whether he were alive or not."

"Perhaps you will see him again some time."

"I don't know. I used to think so; but I have about given up hopes of it. It is six years now since he ran away."

"Maybe he's turned bad," said Ben. "S'posin' he was a ragged baggage-smasher like me, you wouldn't care about seein' him, would you?"

"Yes, I would," said Charles, warmly. "I'd be glad to see Ben again, no matter how he looked, or how poor he might be."

Ben looked at his cousin with a glance of wistful affection. Street boy as he was, old memories had been awakened, and his heart had been touched by the sight of the cousin whom he had most loved when a young boy.

"And I might be like him," thought Ben, looking askance at the rags in which he was dressed, "instead of a walkin' rag-bag. I wish I was;" and he suppressed a sigh.

It has been said that street boys are not accessible to the softer emotions; but Ben did long to throw his arm round his cousin's neck in the old, affectionate way of six years since. It touched him to think that Charlie held him in affectionate remembrance. But his thoughts were diverted by noticing that they had reached the Astor House.

"I guess we'd better cross the street, and take the Fourth Avenue cars," he said. "There's one over there."

"All right!" said Charles. "I suppose you know best."

There was a car just starting; they succeeded in getting aboard, and were speedily on their up town.

CHAPTER XVII

BEN FORMS A RESOLUTION

"Does this car go up Madison Avenue?" asked Charles, after they had taken their seats.

"No," said Ben, "it goes up Fourth Avenue; but that's only one block away from Madison. We'll get out at Thirtieth Street."

"I'm glad you're with me; I might have a hard time finding the place if I were alone."

"Are you going to stay in the city long?" asked Ben.

"Yes, I am going to school here. Father is going to move here soon. Until he comes I shall stay with my Cousin Mary."

Ben felt quite sure that this must be his older sister, but did not like to ask.

"Is she married?"

"Yes, it is the sister of my Cousin Ben. About two years ago she married a New York gentleman. He is a broker, and has an office in Wall Street. I suppose he's rich."

"What's his name?" asked Ben. "Maybe I've seen his office."

"It is Abercrombie,—James Abercrombie. Did you ever hear that name?"

"No," answered Ben, "I can't say as I have. He aint the broker that does my business."

"Have you much business for a broker?" asked Charles, laughing.

"I do a smashin' business in Erie and New York Central," answered Ben.

"You are in the same business as the railroads," said Charles.

"How is that?"

"You are both baggage-smashers."

"That's so; only I don't charge so much for smashin' baggage as they do."

They were on Centre Street now, and a stone building with massive stone columns came in view on the west side of the street.

"What building is that?" asked Charles.

"That's a hotel, where they lodge people free gratis."

Charles looked at his companion for information.

"It's the Tombs," said Ben. "It aint so popular, though, as the hotels where they charge higher."

"No, I suppose not. It looks gloomy enough."

"It aint very cheerful," said Ben. "I never put up there, but that's what people say that have enjoyed that privilege."

"Where is the Bowery?"

"We'll soon be in it. We turn off Centre Street a little farther up."

Charles was interested in all that he saw. The broad avenue which is known as the Bowery, with its long line of shops on either side, and the liberal display of goods on the sidewalk, attracted his attention, and he had numerous questions to ask, most of which Ben was able to answer. He had not knocked about the streets of New York six years for nothing. His business had carried him to all parts of the city, and he had acquired a large amount of local information, a part of which he retailed now to his cousin as they rode side by side in the horse-cars.

At length they reached Thirtieth Street, and here they got out. At the distance of one block they found Madison Avenue. Examining the numbers, they readily found the house of which they were in search. It was a handsome four-story house, with a brown-stone front.

"This must be Mr. Abercrombie's house," said Charles. "I didn't think Cousin Mary lived in such a nice place."

Ben surveyed the house with mingled emotions. He could not help contrasting his own forlorn, neglected condition with the position of his sister. She lived in an elegant home, enjoying, no doubt, all the advantages which money could procure; while he, her only brother, walked about the streets in rags, sleeping in any out-of-the-way corner. But he could blame no one for it. It had been his own choice, and until this morning he had been well enough contented with it. But all at once a glimpse had been given him of what might have been his lot had he been less influenced by pride and waywardness, and by the light of this new prospect he saw how little hope there was of achieving any decent position in society if he remained in his present occupation. But what could he do? Should he declare himself at once to his cousin, and his sister? Pride would not permit him to do it. He was not willing to let them see him in his ragged and dirty state. He determined to work and save up money, until he could purchase a suit as handsome as that which his cousin wore. Then he would not be ashamed to present himself, so far as his outward appearance went. He knew very well that he was ignorant; but he must trust to the future to remedy that deficiency. It would be a work of time, as he well knew. Meanwhile he had his cousin's assurance that he would be glad to meet him again, and renew the old, affectionate intimacy which formerly existed between them.

While these thoughts were passing through Ben's mind, as I have said, they reached the house.

"Have you had any breakfast?" asked Charles as they ascended the steps.

"Not yet," answered Ben. "It isn't fashionable to take breakfast early."

"Then you must come in. My cousin will give you some breakfast."

Ben hesitated; but finally decided to accept the invitation. He had two reasons for this. Partly because it would give him an opportunity to see his sister; and, secondly, because it would save him the expense of buying his breakfast elsewhere, and that was a consideration, now that he had a special object for saving money.

"Is Mrs. Abercrombie at home?" asked Charles of the servant who answered his summons.

"Yes, sir; who shall I say is here?"

"Her cousin, Charles Montrose."

"Will you walk into the parlor?" said the servant, opening a door at the side of the hall. She looked doubtfully at Ben, who had also entered the house.

"Sit down here, Ben," said Charles, indicating a chair on one side of the hat-stand. "I'll stop here till Mrs. Abercrombie comes down," he said.

Soon a light step was heard on the stairs, and Mrs. Abercrombie descended the staircase. She is the same that we last saw in the modest house in the Pennsylvania village; but the lapse of time has softened her manners, and the influence of a husband and a home have improved her. But otherwise she has not greatly changed in her looks.

Ben, who examined her face eagerly, recognized her at once. Yes, it was his sister Mary that stood before him. He would have known her anywhere. But there was a special mark by which he remembered her. There was a dent in her cheek just below the temple, the existence of which he could account for. In a fit of boyish passion, occasioned by her teasing him, he had flung a stick of wood at her head, and this had led to the mark.

"Where did you come from, Charles?" she said, giving her hand cordially to her young cousin.

"From Boston, Cousin Mary."

"Have you just arrived, and where is your father? You did not come on alone, did you?"

"No, father is with me, or rather he came on with me, but he had some errands down town, and stopped to attend to them. He will be here soon."

"How did you find the way alone?"

"I was not alone. There is my guide. By the way, I told him to stay, and you would give him some breakfast."

"Certainly, he can go down in the basement, and the servants will give him something."

Mrs. Abercrombie looked at Ben as she spoke; but on her part there was no sign of recognition. This was not strange. A boy changes greatly between ten and sixteen years of age, and when to this natural change is added the great change in Ben's dress, it will not be wondered at that his sister saw in him only an ordinary street boy.

Ben was relieved to find that he was not known. He had felt afraid that something in his looks might remind his sister of her lost brother; but the indifferent look which she turned upon him proved that he had no ground for this fear.

"You have not breakfasted, I suppose, Charles." said his cousin.

"You wouldn't think so, if you knew what an appetite I have," he answered, laughing.

"We will do our best to spoil it," said Mrs. Abercrombie.

She rang the bell, and ordered breakfast to be served.

"We are a little late this morning," she said.

"Mr. Abercrombie is in Philadelphia on business; so you won't see him till to-morrow."

When the servant appeared, Mrs. Abercrombie directed her to take Ben downstairs, and give him something to eat.

"Don't go away till I see you, Ben," said Charles, lingering a little.

"All right," said Ben.

He followed the servant down the stairs leading to the basement. On the way, he had a glimpse through the half-open door of the breakfast-table, at which his sister and his cousin were shortly to sit down.

"Some time, perhaps, I shall be invited in there," he said to himself.

But at present he had no such wish. He knew that in his ragged garb he would be out of place in the handsome breakfast-room, and he preferred to wait until his appearance was improved. He had no fault to find with the servants, who brought him a bountiful supply of beefsteak and bread and butter, and a cup of excellent coffee. Ben had been up long enough to have quite an appetite. Besides, the quality of the breakfast was considerably superior to those which he was accustomed to take in the cheap restaurants which he frequented, and he did full justice to the food that was spread before him.

When he had satisfied his appetite, he had a few minutes to wait before Charles came down to speak to him.

"Well, Ben, I hope you had a good breakfast," he said.

"Tip-top," answered Ben.

"And I hope also that you had an appetite equal to mine."

"My appetite don't often give out," said Ben; "but it aint so good now as it was when I came in."

"Now we have a little business to attend to. How much shall I pay you for smashing my baggage?" Charles asked, with a laugh.

"Whatever you like."

"Well, here's fifty cents for your services, and six cents for your car-fare back."

"Thank you," said Ben.

"Besides this, Mrs. Abercrombie has a note, which she wants carried down town to her husband's office in Wall Street. She will give you fifty cents more, if you will agree to deliver it there at once, as it is of importance."

"All right," said Ben. "I'll do it."

"Here is the note. I suppose you had better start with it at once. Good-morning."

"Good-morning," said Ben, as he held his cousin's proffered hand a moment in his own. "Maybe I'll see you again some time."

"I hope so," said Charles, kindly.

A minute later Ben was on his way to take a Fourth Avenue car down town.

CHAPTER XVIII

LUCK AND ILL LUCK

"That will do very well for a beginning," thought Ben, as he surveyed, with satisfaction, the two half dollars which he had received for his morning's services. He determined to save one of them towards the fund which he hoped to accumulate for the object which he had in view. How much he would need he could not decide; but thought that it would be safe to set the amount at fifty dollars. This would doubtless require a considerable time to obtain. He could not expect to be so fortunate every day as he had been this morning. Some days, no doubt, he would barely earn enough to pay expenses. Still he had made a beginning, and this was something gained. It was still more encouraging that he had determined to save money, and had an inducement to do so.

As Ben rode down town in the horse-cars, he thought of the six years which he had spent as a New York street boy; and he could not help feeling that the time had been wasted, so far as any progress or improvement was concerned. Of books he knew less than when he first came to the city. He knew more of life, indeed, but not the best side of life. He had formed some bad habits, from which he would probably have been saved if he had remained at home. Ben realized all at once how much he had lost by his hasty action in leaving home. He regarded his street life with different eyes, and felt ready to give it up, as soon as he could present himself to his parents without too great a sacrifice of his pride.

At the end of half an hour, Ben found himself at the termination of the car route, opposite the lower end of the City Hall Park.

As the letter which he had to deliver was to be carried to Wall Street, he kept on down Broadway till he reached Trinity Church, and then turned into the street opposite. He quickly found the number indicated, and entered Mr. Abercrombie's office. It was a handsome office on the lower floor. Two or three clerks were at work at their desks.

"So this is my brother-in-law's office," thought Ben. "It's rather better than mine."

"Well, young man, what can I do for you to-day?" inquired a

clerk, in a tone which indicated that he thought Ben had got into the wrong shop.

"You can tell me whether your name is Sampson," answered Ben, coolly.

"No, it isn't."

"That's what I thought."

"Suppose I am not; what then?"

"Then the letter I've got isn't for you, that's all."

"So you've got a letter, have you?"

"That's what I said."

"It seems to me you're mighty independent," sneered the clerk, who felt aggrieved that Ben did not show him the respect which he conceived to be his due.

"Thank you for the compliment," said Ben, bowing.

"You can hand me the letter."

"I thought your name wasn't Sampson."

"I'll hand it to Mr. Sampson. He's gone out a moment. He'll be in directly."

"Much obliged," said Ben; "but I'd rather hand it to Mr. Sampson myself. Business aint particularly pressin' this mornin', so, if you'll hand me the mornin' paper, I'll read till he comes."

"Well, you've got cheek," ejaculated the clerk.

"I've got two of 'em if I counted right when I got up," said Ben.

Here there was a laugh from the other two clerks.

"He's too smart for you, Granby," said one.

"He's impudent enough," muttered the first, as he withdrew discomfited to his desk.

The enemy having retreated, Ben sat down in an arm-chair, and, picking up a paper, began to read.

He had not long to wait. Five minutes had scarcely passed when a man of middle age entered the office. His manner showed that he belonged there.

"If you're Mr. Sampson," said Ben, approaching him, "here is a letter for you."

"That is my name," said the gentleman, opening the note at once.

"You come from Mrs. Abercrombie," he said, glancing at Ben, as he finished reading it.

"Yes, sir," said Ben.

"How did she happen to select you as her messenger?"

"I went up there this morning to carry a valise."

"I have a great mind to send you back to her with an answer; but I hesitate on one account."

"What is that?" asked Ben.

"I don't know whether you can be trusted."

"Nor I," said Ben; "but I'm willin' to run the risk."

"No doubt," said Mr. Sampson, smiling; "but it seems to me that I should run a greater risk than you."

"I don't know about that," answered Ben. "If it's money, and I keep it, you can send the cops after me, and I'll be sent to the Island. That would be worse than losing money."

"That's true; but some of you boys don't mind that. However, I am inclined to trust you. Mrs. Abercrombie asks for a sum of money, and wishes me to send it up by one of the clerks. That I cannot very well do, as we are particularly busy this morning. I will put the money in an envelope, and give it to you to deliver. I will tell you beforehand that it is fifty dollars."

"Very good," said Ben; "I'll give it to her."

"Wait a moment."

Mr. Sampson went behind the desk, and reappeared almost directly.

"Mrs. Abercrombie will give you a line to me, stating that she has received the money. When you return with this, I will pay you for your trouble."

"All right," said Ben.

As he left the office the young clerk first mentioned said, "I am afraid, Mr. Sampson, Mrs. Abercrombie will never see that money."

"Why not?"

"The boy will keep it."

"What makes you think so?"

"He's one of the most impudent young rascals I ever saw."

"I didn't form that opinion. He was respectful enough to me."

"He wasn't to me."

Mr. Sampson smiled a little. He had observed young Granby's assumption of importance, and partly guessed how matters stood.

"It's too late to recall him," he said. "I must run the risk. My own opinion is that he will prove faithful."

Ben had accepted the commission gladly, not alone because he would get extra pay for the additional errand, but because he saw that there was some hesitation in the mind of Mr. Sampson about trusting him, and he meant to show himself worthy of confidence. There were fifty dollars in the envelope. He had never before been trusted with that amount of money, and now it was rather because no other messenger could be conveniently sent that he found himself so trusted. Not a thought of appropriating the money came to Ben. True, it occurred to him that this was precisely the sum which he needed to fit him out respectably. But there would be greater cause for shame if he appeared well dressed on stolen money, than if he should present himself in rags to his sister. However, it is only just to Ben to say that had the party to whom he was sent been different, he would have discharged his commission honorably. Not that he was a model boy, but his pride, which was in some respects a fault with him, here served him in good stead, as it made him ashamed to do a dishonest act.

Ben rightly judged that the money would be needed as soon as possible, and, as the distance was great, he resolved to ride, trusting to Mr. Sampson's liberality to pay him for the expense which he would thus incur in addition to the compensation allowed for his services.

He once more made his way to the station of the Fourth Avenue cars, and jumped aboard one just ready to start.

The car gradually filled, and they commenced their progress up town.

Ben took a seat in the corner next to the door. Next to him was a man with black hair and black whiskers. He wore a tall felt hat with a bell crown, and a long cloak. Ben took no particular notice of him, being too much in the habit of seeing strange faces to observe them minutely. The letter he put in the side pocket of his coat, on the side nearest the stranger. He took it out once to look at it. It was addressed to Mrs. Abercrombie, at her residence, and in one corner Mr. Sampson had written "Money enclosed."

Now it chanced, though Ben did not suspect it, that the man at his side was a member of the swell mob, and his main business was picking pockets. He observed the two words, already quoted, on the envelope when Ben took it in his hand, and he made up his mind to get possession of it. This was comparatively easy, for Ben's pocket was on the side towards him. Our hero was rather careless, it must be owned, but it happened that the inside pocket of his coat had been torn away, which left him no other receptacle for the letter. Besides, Ben had never been in a situation to have much fear of pick pockets, and under ordinary circumstances he would hardly have been selected as worth plundering. But the discovery that the letter contained money altered the case.

While Ben was looking out from the opposite window across the street, the stranger dexterously inserted his hand in his pocket, and withdrew the letter. They were at that moment just opposite the Tombs.

Having gained possession of the letter, of course it was his interest to get out of the car as soon as possible, since Ben was liable at any moment to discover his loss.

He touched the conductor, who was just returning from the other end of the car, after collecting the fares.

"I'll get out here," he said.

The conductor accordingly pulled the strap, and the car stopped.

The stranger gathered his cloak about him, and, stepping out on the platform, jumped from the car. Just at that moment Ben put his hand into his pocket, and instantly discovered the loss of the letter. He immediately connected it with the departure of his fellow-passenger, and, with a hasty ejaculation, sprang from the car, and started in pursuit of him.

CHAPTER XIX

WHICH IS THE GUILTY PARTY?

It was an exciting moment for Ben. He felt that his character for honesty was at stake. In case the pickpocket succeeded in getting off with the letter and money, Mr. Sampson would no doubt come to the conclusion that he had appropriated the fifty dollars to his own use, while his story of the robbery would be regarded as an impudent fabrication. He might even be arrested, and sentenced to the Island for theft. If this should happen, though he were innocent, Ben felt that he should not be willing to make himself known to his sister or his parents. But there was a chance of getting back the money, and he resolved to do his best.

The pickpocket turned down a side street, his object being to get out of the range of observation as soon as possible. But one thing he did not anticipate, and this was Ben's immediate discovery of his loss. On this subject he was soon enlightened. He saw Ben jump from the horse-car, and his first impulse was to run. He made a quick movement in advance, and then paused. It occurred to him that he occupied a position of advantage with regard to his accuser, being respectably dressed, while Ben was merely a ragged street boy, whose word probably would not inspire much confidence. This vantage ground he would give up by having recourse to flight, as this would be a virtual acknowledgment of guilt. He resolved instantaneously to assume an attitude of conscious integrity, and frown down upon Ben from the heights of assumed respectability. There was one danger, however, that he was known to some of the police force in his true character. But he must take the risk of recognition.

On landing in the middle of the street, Ben lost no time; but, running up to the pickpocket, caught him by the arm.

"What do you want, boy?" he demanded, in a tone of indifference.

"I want my money," said Ben.

"I don't understand you," said the pickpocket loftily.

"Look here, mister," said Ben, impatiently; "you know well enough what I mean. You took a letter with money in it out of my pocket. Just hand it back, and I won't say anything about it."

"You're an impudent young rascal," returned the "gentleman," affecting to be outraged by such a charge. "Do you dare to accuse a gentleman like me of robbing a ragmuffin like you?"

"Yes, I do," said Ben, boldly.

"Then you're either crazy or impudent, I don't know which."

"Call me what you please; but give me back my money."

"I don't believe you ever had five dollars in your possession. How much do you mean to say there was in this letter?"

"Fifty dollars," answered Ben.

The pickpocket had an object in asking this question. He wanted to learn whether the sum of money was sufficient to make it worth his while to keep it. Had it been three or four dollars, he might have given it up, to avoid risk and trouble. But on finding that it was fifty dollars he determined to hold on to it at all hazards.

"Clear out, boy," he said, fiercely. "I shan't stand any of your impudence."

"Give me my money, then."

"If you don't stop that, I'll knock you down," repeated the pickpocket, shaking off Ben's grasp, and moving forward rapidly.

If he expected to frighten our hero away thus easily, he was very much mistaken. Ben had too much at stake to give up the attempt to recover the letter. He ran forward, and, seizing the man by the arm, he reiterated, in a tone of firm determination, "Give me my money, or I'll call a copp."

"Take that, you young villain!" exclaimed the badgered thief, bringing his fist in contact with Ben's face in such a manner as to cause the blood to flow.

In a physical contest it was clear that Ben would get the worst of it. He was but a boy of sixteen, strong, indeed, of his age; but still what could he expect to accomplish against a tall man of mature age? He saw that he needed help, and he called out at the top of his lungs, "Help! Police!"

His antagonist was adroit, and a life spent in eluding the law had made him quick-witted. He turned the tables upon Ben by turning round, grasping him firmly by the arm, and repeating in a voice louder than Ben's, "Help! Police!"

Contrary to the usual custom in such cases, a policeman happened to be near, and hurried to the spot where he was apparently wanted.

"What's the row?" he asked.

Before Ben had time to prefer his charge, the pickpocket said glibly:—

"Policeman, I give this boy in charge."

"What's he been doing?"

"I caught him with his hand in my pocket," said the man. "He's a thieving young vagabond."

"That's a lie!" exclaimed Ben, rather startled at the unexpected turn which affairs had taken. "He's a pickpocket."

The real culprit shrugged his shoulders. "You aint quite smart enough, boy," he said.

"Has he taken anything of yours?" asked the policeman, who supposed Ben to be what he was represented.

"No," said the pickpocket; "but he came near taking a money letter which I have in my pocket."

Here, with astonishing effrontery, he displayed the letter which he had stolen from Ben.

"That's *my* letter," said Ben. "He took it from my pocket."

"A likely story," smiled the pickpocket, in serene superiority. "The letter is for Mrs. Abercrombie, a friend of mine, and contains fifty dollars. I incautiously wrote upon the envelope 'Money enclosed,' which attracted the attention of this young vagabond, as I held it in my hand. On replacing it in my pocket, he tried to get possession of it."

"That's a lie from beginning to end," exclaimed Ben, impetuously. "He's tryin' to make me out a thief, when he's one himself."

"Well, what is your story?" asked the policeman, who, however, had already decided in his own mind that Ben was the guilty party.

"I was ridin' in the Fourth Avenue cars along side of this man," said Ben, "when he put his hand in my pocket, and took out the letter that he's just showed you. I jumped out after him, and asked him to give it back, when he fetched me a lick in the face."

"Do you mean to say that a ragamuffin like you had fifty dollars?" demanded the thief.

"No," said Ben, "the money wasn't mine. I was carryin' it up to Mrs. Abercrombie, who lives on Madison Avenue."

"It's a likely story that a ragamuffin like you would be trusted with so much money."

"If you don't believe it," said Ben, "go to Mr. Abercrombie's office in Wall Street. Mr. Sampson gave it to me only a few minutes ago. If he says he didn't, just carry me to the station-house as quick as you want to."

This confident assertion of Ben's put matters in rather a different light. It seemed straightforward, and the reference might easily prove which was the real culprit. The pickpocket saw that the officer wavered, and rejoined hastily, "You must expect the officer's a fool to believe your ridiculous story."

"It's not so ridiculous," answered the policeman, scrutinizing the speaker with sudden suspicion. "I am not sure but the boy is right."

"I'm willing to let the matter drop," said the pickpocket, magnanimously; "as he didn't succeed in getting my money, I will not prosecute. You may let him go, Mr. Officer."

"Not so fast," said the policeman, his suspicions of the other party getting stronger and more clearly defined. "I haven't any authority to do as you say."

"Very well, take him along then. I suppose the law must take its course."

"Yes, it must."

"Very well, boy, I'm sorry you've got into such a scrape; but it's your own fault. Good morning, officer."

"You're in too much of a hurry," said the policeman, coolly; "you must go along with me too."

"Really," said the thief, nervously, "I hope you'll excuse me. I've got an important engagement this morning, and—I—in fact it will be excessively inconvenient."

"I'm sorry to put you to inconvenience, but it can't be helped."

"Really, Mr. Officer—"

"It's no use. I shall need you. Oblige me by handing me that letter."

"Here it is," said the thief, unwillingly surrendering it. "Really, it's excessively provoking. I'd rather lose the money than break my engagement. I'll promise to be on hand at the trial, whenever it comes off; if you keep the money it will be a guaranty of my appearance."

"I don't know about that," answered the officer "As to being present at the trial, I mean that you shall be."

"Of course, I promised that."

"There's one little matter you seem to forget, said the officer; "your appearance may be quite as necessary as the boy's. It may be your trial and not his."

"Do you mean to insult me?" demanded the pickpocket, haughtily.

"Not by no manner of means. I aint the judge, you know. If your story is all right, it'll appear so."

"Of course; but I shall have to break my engagement."

"Well, that can't be helped as I see. Come along, if *you* please."

He tucked one arm in that of the man, and the other in Ben's, and moved towards the station-house. Of the two Ben seemed to be much the more unconcerned. He was confident that his innocence would be proclaimed, while the other was equally convinced that trouble awaited him.

"Well, boy, how do you like going to the station-house?" asked the policeman.

"I don't mind as long as he goes with me," answered Ben. "What I was most afraid of was that I'd lose the money, and then Mr. Sampson would have taken me for a thief."

Meanwhile the other party was rapidly getting more and more nervous. He felt that he was marching to his fate, and that the only way of escape was by flight, and that immediate; for they were very near the station-house. Just as Ben pronounced the last words, the thief gathered all his strength, and broke from the grasp of the officer, whose hold was momentarily relaxed. Once free he showed an astonishing rapidity.

The officer hesitated for an instant, for he had another prisoner to guard.

"Go after him," exclaimed Ben, eagerly. "Don't let him escape. I'll stay where I am."

The conviction that the escaped party was the real thief determined the policeman to follow Ben's advice. He let him go, and started in rapid pursuit of the fugitive.

Ben sat down on a doorstep, and awaited anxiously the result of the chase.

CHAPTER XX

HOW ALL CAME RIGHT IN THE MORNING

It is quite possible that the pickpocket would have made good his escape, if he had not, unluckily for himself, run into another policeman.

"Beg your pardon," he said, hurriedly.

"Stop a minute," said the officer, detaining him by the arm, for his appearance and haste inspired suspicion. He was bare-headed, for his hat had fallen off, and he had not deemed it prudent to stop long enough to pick it up.

"I'm in a great hurry," panted the thief. "My youngest child is in a fit, and I am running for a physician."

This explanation seemed plausible, and the policeman, who was himself the father of a family, was on the point of releasing him, when the first officer came up.

"Hold on to him," he said; "he's just broken away from me."

"That's it, is it?" said the second policeman. "He told me he was after a doctor for his youngest child."

"I think he'll need a doctor himself," said the first, "if he tries another of his games. You didn't stop to say good-by, my man."

"I told you I had an important engagement," said the pickpocket, sulkily,—"one that I cared more about than the money. Where's the boy?"

"I had to leave him to go after you."

"That's a pretty way to manage; you let the thief go in order to chase his victim."

"You're an able-bodied victim," said the policeman, laughing.

"Where are you taking me?"

"I'm going back for the boy. He said he'd wait till I returned."

"Are you green enough to think you'll find him?" sneered the man in charge.

"Perhaps not; but I shouldn't be surprised if I did. If I guess right, he'll find it worth his while to keep his promise."

When they returned to the place where the thief had first effected his escape, our hero was found quietly sitting on a wooden step.

"So you've got him," said Ben, advancing to meet the officer with evident satisfaction.

"He's got you too," growled the pickpocket. "Why didn't you run away, you little fool?"

"I didn't have anything to run for," answered Ben. "Besides, I want my money back."

"Then you'll have to go with me to the station-house," said the officer.

"I wish I could go to Mr. Abercrombie's office first to tell Mr. Sampson what's happened."

"I can't let you do that; but you may write a letter from the station-house."

"All right," said Ben, cheerfully; and he voluntarily placed himself on the other side of the officer, and accompanied him to the station-house.

"I thought you was guilty at first," said the officer; "but I guess your story is correct. If it isn't, you're about the coolest chap I ever saw, and I've seen some cool ones in my day."

"It's just as I said," said Ben. "It'll all come right in the morning."

They soon reached the station-house. Ben obtained the privilege of writing a letter to Mr. Sampson, for which the officer undertook to procure a messenger. In fact he began to feel quite interested for our hero, feeling fully convinced that the other party was the real offender.

Ben found some difficulty in writing his letter. When he first came to the city, he could have written one with considerable ease, but he had scarcely touched a pen, or formed a letter, for six years, and of course this made an important difference. However he finally managed to write these few lines with a lead-pencil:—

"Mr. Sampson: I am sory I can't cary that leter til to-morrow; but it was took from my pokit by a thefe wen I was ridin' in the cars, and as he sed I took it from him, the 'copp' has brort us both to the stashun-house, whare I hope you wil come and tel them how it was, and that you give me the leter to cary, for the other man says it is his The 'copp' took the leter

"Ben Hooper."

It will be observed that Ben's spelling had suffered; but this will not excite surprise, considering how long it was since he had attended school. It will also be noticed that he did not sign his real name, but used the same which he had communicated to Charles Marston. More than ever, till he was out of his present difficulty, he desired to conceal his identity from his relations.

Meanwhile, Mr. Sampson was busily engaged in his office in Wall

Street. It may as well be explained here that he was the junior partner of Mr. Abercrombie. Occasionally he paused in his business to wonder whether he had done well to expose a ragged street boy to such a temptation; but he was a large-hearted man, inclined to think well of his fellow-men, and though in his business life he had seen a good deal that was mean and selfish in the conduct of others, he had never lost his confidence in human nature, and never would. It is better to have such a disposition, even if it does expose the possessor to being imposed upon at times, than to regard everybody with distrust and suspicion. At any rate it promotes happiness, and conciliates good-will, and these will offset an occasional deception.

An hour had passed, when a boy presented himself at Mr. Abercrombie's office. It was a newsboy, who had been entrusted with Ben's letter.

"This is for Mr. Sampson," he said, looking around him on entering.

"Another of Mr. Sampson's friends," sneered Granby, in a tone which he took care should be too low to come to that gentleman's ears.

"My name is Sampson," said the owner of that name. "Who is your letter from?"

"It's from Ben."

"And who is Ben?" asked Mr. Sampson, not much enlightened.

"It's Ben, the baggage-smasher."

"Give it to me," said the gentleman, conjecturing rightly that it was his messenger who was meant.

He ran his eye rapidly over the paper, or, I should say, as rapidly as the character of Ben's writing would permit.

"Do you come from the station-house?" he asked, looking up.

"Yes, sir."

"Which station-house is it?"

"In Leonard Street."

"Very well. Go back and tell the boy that I will call this afternoon. I will also give you a line to a house on Madison Avenue. Can you go right up there, calling at the station-house on the way?"

"Yes, sir."

"Very well. Here is something for your trouble."

The boy pocketed with satisfaction the money proffered him, and took the letter which Mr. Sampson hastily wrote. It was to this effect:—

"My dear Mrs. Abercrombie: I received your note, and dispatched the money which you desired by a messenger; but I have just learned that his pocket was picked on the horse-cars. I cannot spare one of my clerks just now, but at one o'clock will send one up with the money, hoping that he may have better fortune than the first messenger, and that you will not be seriously inconvenienced by the delay.

"Yours truly,

"Henry Sampson".

Then he dismissed the matter from his mind until afternoon, when, the office having closed, he made his way to the Leonard Street station-house, where he was speedily admitted to see Ben.

"I'm glad you've come, Mr. Sampson," said our hero, eagerly. "I hope you don't think I was to blame about the letter."

"Tell me how it was, my lad," said Mr. Sampson, kindly. "I dare say you can give me a satisfactory explanation."

Ben felt grateful for the kindness of his tone. He saw that he was not condemned unheard, but had a chance of clearing himself.

He explained, briefly, how it occurred. Of course it is unnecessary to give his account, for we know all about it already.

"I believe you," said Mr. Sampson, in a friendly tone. "The only fault I have to find with you is that you might have been more careful in guarding your pockets."

"That's so," said Ben; "but I don't often carry anything that's worth stealing."

"No, I suppose not," said Mr. Sampson, smiling. "Well, it appears that no serious loss has occurred. The money will be recovered, as it is in the hands of the authorities. As to the delay, that is merely an inconvenience; but the most serious inconvenience falls upon you, in your being brought here."

"I don't mind that as long as the money is safe," said Ben. "It'll all be right in the morning."

"I see you are a philosopher. I see your face is swelled. You must have got a blow."

"Yes," said Ben; "the chap that took my letter left me something to remember him by."

"I shall try to make it up to you," said Mr. Sampson. "I can't stop any longer, but I will be present at your trial, and my testimony will undoubtedly clear you."

He took his leave, leaving Ben considerably more cheerful than before. A station-house is not a very agreeable place of detention; but then Ben was not accustomed to luxury, and the absence of comfort did not trouble him much. He cared more for the loss of his liberty, finding the narrow cell somewhat too restricted for enjoyment. However, he consoled himself by reflecting, to use his favorite phrase, that it would "all be right in the morning."

It will not be necessary to give a circumstantial account of Ben's trial. Mr. Sampson was faithful to his promise, and presented himself, somewhat to his personal inconvenience, at the early hour assigned for trial. His testimony was brief and explicit, and cleared Ben. The real pickpocket, however, being recognized by the judge as one who had been up before him some months before, charged with a similar offence, was sentenced to a term of imprisonment, considerably to his dissatisfaction.

Ben left the court-room well pleased with the result. His innocence had been established, and he had proved that he could be trusted, or rather, he had not proved faithless to his trust, and he felt that with his present plans and hopes he could not afford to lose his character for honesty. He knew that he had plenty of faults, but at any rate he was not a thief.

While he stood on the steps of the Tombs, in which the trial had taken place, Mr. Sampson advanced towards him, and touched him on the shoulder.

"Well, my lad," he said, in a friendly manner, "so you're all right once more?"

"Yes," said Ben; "I knew it would all be right in the morning."

"I owe you something for the inconvenience you have suffered while in my employ. Here is a ten-dollar bill. I hope you will save it till you need it, and won't spend it foolishly."

"Thank you," said Ben, joyfully. "I'll put it in the bank."

"That will be a good plan. Good-morning; when you need a friend, you will know where to find me."

He shook Ben's hand in a friendly way and left him.

"He's a trump," thought Ben. "If my father'd treated me like that, I'd never have wanted to run away from home."

CHAPTER XXI

IN A NEW LINE

"Ten dollars!" said Ben to himself, with exultation. "That's pretty good pay for a few hours in the station-house. I'd like to board there a week on the same terms."

Ben's capital now amounted to eleven dollars; but of this sum he decided to retain one dollar as a reserve to fall back upon in case of need. The ten dollars he determined to deposit at once in a savings-bank. He accordingly bent his steps towards one in the course of the forenoon. The business was quickly transacted, and Ben left the building with a bank-book containing an entry of his first deposit.

This was a very good beginning, so Ben thought. Fifty dollars, as he had estimated, would enable him to carry out the plan which he proposed, and he had already one-fifth of the sum. But the accumulation of the other forty dollars would no doubt take him a considerable time. The business of a "baggage-smasher," as Ben knew from experience, is precarious, the amount of gains depending partly upon luck. He had sometimes haunted the steamboat landings for hours without obtaining a single job. Now that he was anxious to get on, he felt this to be an objection. He began to consider whether there was any way of adding to his income.

After considerable thought he decided to buy a supply of weekly papers, which he could sell while waiting for a job. One advantage in selecting weekly papers rather than daily was this, that the latter must be sold within a few hours, or they prove a dead loss. A daily paper of yesterday is as unsalable as a last year's almanac. As Ben was liable to be interrupted in his paper business at any time by a chance to carry luggage, it was an important consideration to have a stock which would remain fresh for a few days.

This idea impressed Ben so favorably that he determined to act upon it at once. In considering where he should go for his supply of papers, he thought of a Broadway news-stand, which he frequently had occasion to pass. On reaching it, he said to the proprietor, "Where do you buy your papers?"

"What do you want to know for?"

"I thought maybe I'd go into the business."

"You don't think of setting up a stand, do you?" asked the man, with a significant glance at Ben's ragged attire.

"No," said Ben. "I haven't got capital enough for that, unless you'll sell out for fifty cents."

"I suppose you want a few to carry round and sell?"

"Yes."

"Where do you think of going with them?"

"Down to the wharves. I'm a baggage-smasher, and I thought I might make somethin' by sellin' papers, when I hadn't any baggage to carry."

"I get my papers from the 'American News Company' on Nassau Street."

"I know the place well enough."

"What papers do you think I could sell best?" asked Ben.

"The picture papers go off as fast as any," said the street dealer. "But I'll tell you what, my lad, maybe I can make an arrangement for you to sell papers for me."

"I don't think I'd like to stand here all day," said Ben, supposing the other to mean to engage him to tend the stand.

"I don't mean that."

"Well, said Ben, "I'm open to an offer, as the old maid of sixty told a feller that called to see her."

"I'll tell you what I mean. I'll give you a bundle of papers every morning to take with you. You will sell what you can, and bring back the rest at night."

"I like that," said Ben, with satisfaction. "But how much will I get?"

"It will depend on the price of the papers. 'Harper's Weekly' and 'Frank Leslie' sell for ten cents. I will allow you two cents on each of these. On the 'Ledger' and 'Weekly,' and other papers of that price, I will allow one cent. You'd make rather more if you bought them yourself; but you might have them left on your hands."

"That's so," said Ben.

"Did you ever sell papers?"

"I used to sell the mornin' and evenin' papers before I went to baggage-smashin'."

"Then you know something about the business. When do you want to begin?"

"Right off."

"Very well; I will make you up a bundle of a dozen papers to begin on. I'll put in three each of the illustrated papers, and fill up with the story papers."

"All right, mister, you know better than I what people will buy."

The dealer began to collect the papers, but paused in the middle of his task, and looked doubtfully at our hero.

"Well, what's up?" asked Ben, observing his hesitation.

"How do I know but you'll sell the papers, and keep the money yourself?" said the dealer.

"That's so," said Ben. "I never thought of that."

"That wouldn't be very profitable for me, you see."

"I'll bring back the money or the papers," said Ben. "You needn't be afraid."

"Very likely you would; but how am I to know that?"

"So you don't want to trust me," said Ben, rather disappointed.

"Have you got any money?"

"Yes."

"Very well, you can leave enough with me to secure me against loss, and I will give you the papers."

"How much will that be?"

After a little thought, the dealer answered, "Seventy-five cents." He had some doubt whether Ben had so much; but our hero quickly set his doubts at rest by drawing out his two half-dollars, and demanding a quarter in change.

The sight of this money reassured the dealer. Ben's ragged clothes had led him to doubt his financial soundness; but the discovery that he was a capitalist to the extent of a dollar gave him considerable more respect for him. A dollar may not be a very large sum; I hope that to you, my young reader, it is a very small one, and that you have never been embarrassed for the want of it; but it is enough to lift a ragged street boy from the position of a penniless vagabond to that of a thrifty capitalist. After seeing it, the dealer would almost have felt safe in trusting Ben with the papers without demanding a deposit of their value. Still it was better and safer to require a deposit, and he therefore took the dollar from Ben, returning twenty-five cents in change.

This preliminary matter settled, he made up the parcel of papers.

"There they are," he said. "If you're smart, you can sell 'em all before night."

"I hope so," said Ben.

With the papers under his arm, Ben made his way westward to the Cortlandt Street ferry, which was a favorite place of resort with him.

He did not have long to wait for his first customer. As he was

walking down Cortlandt Street, he met a gentleman, whose attention seemed attracted by the papers he carried.

"What papers have you got there, my lad?" he inquired.

"'Harper's Weekly,' 'Frank Leslie,' 'Ledger,' 'Weekly,'" repeated
Ben, glibly, adding the names of the other papers in his parcel.

"Give me the two picture papers," said the gentleman. "Twenty
cents, I suppose."

"Yes," said Ben, "and as much more as you want to pay. I don't
set no limit to the generosity of my customers."

"You're sharp," said the gentleman, laughing. "That's worth
something. Here's twenty-five cents. You may keep the change."

"I'll do it cheerfully," said Ben. "Thank you, sir. I hope you'll buy
all your papers of me."

"I won't promise always to pay you more than the regular price,
but you may leave 'Harper's' and 'Leslie' at my office every week.
Here is my card."

Ben took the card, and put it in his pocket. He found the office
to be located in Trinity Building, Broadway.

"I'll call every week reg'lar," he said.

"That's right, my lad. Good-morning."

"Good-mornin'."

Ben felt that he had started well. He had cleared nine cents by
his sale, four representing his regular commission, while the other
five cents might be regarded as a donation. Nine cents was something. But for his idea about the papers, he would have made
nothing so far. It is a very good thing to have two strings to your
bow, so Ben thought, though the thought did not take that pre-
cise form in his mind. He kept on his way till he reached the ferry.
There was no train in on the other side, and would not be for some
time, but passengers came over the ferry, and Ben placed himself
where he could be seen. It was some time before he sold another
paper however, although Ben, who improved some of his spare
time by looking over the pictures, was prepared to recommend
them.

"What papers have you got, boy? " asked a tall, lank man, whose
thin lips and pinched expression gave him an outward appearance
of meanness, which, by the way, did not belie his real character.

Ben recited the list.

"What's the price of 'Harper's Weekly'?"

"Ten cents."

"Ten cents is too much to pay for any paper. I don't see how they
have the face to ask it."

"Nor I," said Ben; "but they don't consult me,"

"I'll give you eight cents."

"No you won't, not if I know it. I'd rather keep the paper for my private readin'," answered Ben.

"Then you are at liberty to do so," said the gentleman, snappishly. "You'd make profit enough, if you sold at eight cents."

"All the profit I'd make wouldn't pay for a fly's breakfast," said Ben.

The gentleman deigned no response, but walked across the street in a dignified manner. Here he was accosted by a boot-black, who proposed to shine his boots.

"He'll get 'em done at the wholesale price, see if he don't," thought Ben. He kept an eye on the boot-black and his patron until the job was finished. Then he witnessed what appeared to be an angry dispute between the two parties. It terminated by the gentleman lifting his cane in a menacing manner. Ben afterwards gained from the boy particulars of the transaction, which may be given here in the third person.

"Shine yer boots?" asked the boot-black, as the gentleman reached his side of the street, just after his unsuccessful negotiations with Ben.

"What do you charge?" he inquired.

"Ten cents."

"That's too much."

"It's the reg'lar price."

"I can get my boots blacked for five cents anywhere. If you'll do it for that, you can go to work."

The boy hesitated. It was half price, but he had not yet obtained a job, and he yielded. When the task was finished, his generous patron drew four cents from his pocket.

"I haven't got but four cents," he observed. "I guess that'll do."

The boy was indignant, as was natural. To work for half price, and then lose one-fifth of his reduced pay, was aggravating. What made it worse was, that his customer was carefully dressed, and bore every appearance of being a man of substance.

"I want another cent," he demanded.

"You're well enough paid," said the other, drawing on a kid glove. "Four cents I consider very handsome pay for ten minutes' work. Many men do not make as much."

This reasoning did not strike the little boot-black as sound. He was no logician; but he felt that he had been defrauded, and that in a very mean manner.

"Give me my money," he screamed, angrily.

"I'll hand you over to the authorities," said the gentleman,—though I hardly feel justified in calling him such,—lifting his cane menacingly.

What could the boy do? Might was evidently on the side of the man who had cheated him. But he was quick-witted, and a characteristic mode of revenge suggested itself. The street was muddy (New York streets are occasionally in that condition). The boot-black stooped down and clutched a handful of mire in his hand, fortunately having no kid gloves to soil, and, before his late customer fathomed his intention, plentifully besprinkled one of the boots which he had just carefully polished.

"That's worth a cent," he remarked, with satisfaction, escaping from the wrath of the injured party.

His victim, almost speechless with rage, seemed disposed to pursue him; but the boy, regardless of the mire, had run across the street, and to follow would only be to make matters worse.

"If I ever catch you, I'll break every bone in your body, you little vagabond," he said, in a voice almost choked by passion, shaking his cane energetically.

Ben, who had witnessed the whole, burst into a hearty laugh, which drew upon his head a portion of wrath. After a pause, the victim of his own meanness turned up a side street. The reader will be glad to learn that he had to employ a second boot black; so that he was not so much better off for his economical management after all. It may be added that he was actuated in all his dealings by the same frugality, if we may dignify it by that name. He was a large dealer in ready-made under-clothing, for the making of which he paid starvation prices; but, unfortunately, the poor sewing-girls, whom he employed for a pittance, were not so well able to defend themselves against imposition as the smart little boot-black, who "knew his rights, and knowing, dared maintain."

CHAPTER XXII

THE HEAVY VALISE

Ben had sold half his papers when the arrival of the train from Philadelphia gave him an opportunity to return to his legitimate calling.

"Smash your baggage, sir?" asked Ben of a dark-complexioned man of thirty-five, who carried a moderate-sized valise.

"Yes," said the other.

"Where shall I carry it?"

"To——" Here the man hesitated, and finally answered, "There is no need of telling you. I will take it from you when we have got along far enough."

Ben was about to walk beside the owner of the valise; but the latter objected to this.

"You needn't walk beside me," he said. "Keep about a block ahead."

"But how will I know where to go?" asked Ben, naturally.

"You know where Broome Street runs into the Bowery?"

"Of course I do."

"Go there by the shortest route. Don't trouble yourself about me. I'll follow along behind, and take the valise from you there. If you get there before I do, wait for me."

"I suppose I'm too ragged to walk alongside of him," thought Ben.

He could think of no other reason for the direction given by the other. However, Ben's pride was not very much hurt. Although he was ragged now, he did not mean to be long. The time would come, he was confident, when he could lay aside his rags, and appear in a respectable dress.

The valise which he carried proved to be considerably heavier than would have been imagined from its size.

"I wonder what's in it," thought Ben, who found it tugging away at his arms. "If it's shirts they're cast-iron. Maybe they're just comin' in fashion."

However, he did not perplex himself much about this point. Beyond a momentary curiosity, he felt no particular interest in the contents of the valise. The way in which it affected him principally

was, to make him inwardly resolve to ask an extra price, on account of the extra weight.

After walking a while he looked back for the owner of the valise.
But he was not in sight.

"I might carry off his baggage," thought Ben, "without his knowin'
it."

He kept on, however, never doubting that the owner would sooner or later overtake him. If he did not care enough for the valise to
do this, Ben would not be responsible.

He had just shifted the heavy burden from one hand to the other, when he felt himself tapped on the shoulder. Looking round,
he saw that the one who had done this was a quiet-looking man,
of middle size, but with a keen, sharp eye.

"What's wanted?" asked Ben.

"Where did you get that valise, my lad?" asked the new-comer.

"I don't know as that's any of your business," answered Ben,
who didn't perceive the other's right to ask the question.

"Is it yours?"

"Maybe it is."

"Let me lift it a moment."

"Hands off!" said Ben, suspiciously. "Don't try none of your tricks
on me."

The other did not appear to notice this.

"I take it for granted that the valise is not yours," he said. "Now
tell me where you got it from."

There was something of authority in his manner, which led Ben
to think that he had a warrant for asking the question, though he
could not guess his object in doing so.

"I'm a baggage-smasher," answered Ben. "I got this from a man
that came by the Philadelphia train."

"Where is he?"

"I guess he's behind somewheres."

"Where are you carrying the valise?"

"Seems to me you want to know a good deal," said Ben, undecided as to the right of the other to ask so many questions.

"I'll let you into a secret, my lad; but you must keep the secret.
That valise is pretty heavy, isn't it?"

"I'll bet it is."

"To the best of my information, the man who employed you is
a noted burglar, and this valise contains his tools. I am a detective, and am on his track. I received a telegram an hour ago from
Philadelphia, informing me that he was on his way. I got down to

the wharf a little too late. Now tell me where you are to carry this;" and the detective pointed to the valise.

"I am to meet the gentleman at the corner of Broome Street and the Bowery," said Ben.

"Very well. Go ahead and meet him."

"Shall you be there?" asked Ben.

"Never mind. Go on just as if I had not met you, and deliver up the valise."

"If you're goin' to nab him, just wait till I've got my pay. I don't want to smash such heavy baggage for nothin'."

"I agree to that. Moreover, if I succeed in getting hold of the fellow through your information, I don't mind paying you five dollars out of my own pocket."

"Very good," said Ben. "I shan't mind takin' it, not by no means."

"Go on, and don't be in too much of a hurry. I want time to lay my trap."

Ben walked along leisurely, in accordance with his instructions. At length he reached the rendezvous. He found the owner of the valise already in waiting.

"Well, boy," he said, impatiently, "you took your time."

"I generally do," said Ben. "It aint dishonest to take my own time, is it?"

"I've been waiting here for a quarter of an hour. I didn't know but you'd gone to sleep somewhere on the way."

"I don't sleep much in the daytime. It don't agree with my constitution. Well, mister, I hope you'll give me something handsome. Your baggage here is thunderin' heavy."

"There's twenty-five cents," said the other.

"Twenty-five cents!" exclaimed Ben, indignantly.

"Twenty-five cents for walkin' two miles with such a heavy load. It's worth fifty."

"Well, you won't get fifty," said the other, roughly.

"Just get somebody else to carry your baggage next time," said Ben, angrily.

He looked round, and saw the quiet-looking man, before referred to, approaching. He felt some satisfaction in knowing that his recent employer would meet with a check which he was far from anticipating.

Without answering Ben, the latter took the valise, and was about moving away, when the quiet-looking man suddenly quickened his pace, and laid his hand on his arm.

The burglar, for he was really one, started, and turned pale.

"What do you want?"

"You know what I want," said the detective, quietly. "I want you."

"What do you want me for?" demanded the other; but it was easy to see that he was nervous and alarmed.

"You know that also," said the detective; "but I don't mind telling you. You came from Philadelphia this morning, and your name is 'Sly Bill.' You are a noted burglar, and I shall take you into immediate custody."

"You're mistaken," said Bill. "You've got hold of the wrong man."

"That will soon be seen. Have the kindness to accompany me to the station-house, and I'll take a look into that valise of yours."

Bill was physically a stronger man than the detective, but he succumbed at once to the tone of quiet authority with which he spoke, and prepared to follow, though by no means with alacrity.

"Here, my lad," said the detective, beckoning Ben, who came up. "Come and see me at this place, to-morrow," he continued, producing a card, "and I won't forget the promise I made you."

"All right," said Ben.

"I'm in luck ag'in," he said to himself. "At this rate it won't take me long to make fifty dollars. Smashin' baggage for burglars pays pretty well."

He bethought himself of his papers, of which half remained unsold. He sold some on the way back to the wharf, where, after a while, he got another job, for which, being at some distance, he was paid fifty cents.

At five in the afternoon he reported himself at the news-stand.

"I've sold all the papers you gave me," he said, "and here's the money. I guess I can sell more to-morrow."

The news-dealer paid him the commission agreed upon, amounting to eighteen cents, Ben, of course, retaining besides the five cents which had been paid him extra in the morning. This made his earnings for the day ninety-eight cents, besides the dollars promised by the detective.

CHAPTER XXIII

THE SURPRISE

Ben had certainly met with good luck so far. Even his temporary detention at the station-house he regarded as a piece of good luck, since he was paid handsomely for the confinement, while his bed there was considerably more comfortable than he often enjoyed. His adventure with the burglar also brought him in as much as under ordinary circumstances he would have earned in a week. In two days he was able to lay aside fifteen dollars and a half towards his fund.

But of course such lucky adventures could not be expected every day. The bulk of his money must be earned slowly, as the reward of persistent labor and industry. But Ben was willing to work now that he had an object before him. He kept up his double business of baggage-smasher and vender of weekly papers. After a while the latter began to pay him enough to prove quite a help, besides filling up his idle moments. Another good result of his new business was, that, while waiting for customers, he got into the habit of reading the papers he had for sale. Now Ben had done very little reading since he came to New York, and, if called upon to read aloud, would have shown the effects of want of practice, in his frequent blunders. But the daily lessons in reading which he now took began to remedy this deficiency, and give him increased fluency and facility. It also had the effect of making him wish that his education had not been interrupted, so that his Cousin Charles might not be so far ahead of him.

Ben also gave up smoking,—not so much because he considered it injurious, but because cigars cost money, and he was economizing in every possible way. He continued to sleep in the room under the wharf, which thus far the occupants had managed to keep from the knowledge of the police. Gradually the number had increased, until from twenty to thirty boys made it a rendezvous nightly. By some means a stove had been procured, and what was more difficult, got safely down without observation, so that, as the nights grew cooler, the boys managed to make themselves comfortable. Here they talked and told stories, and had a good time before going to sleep. One evening it was proposed by one of the boys that each should tell his own story; for though they met together daily they knew little of each other beyond this, that they were all engaged in some street avocation. Some of the stories told were real, some burlesque.

First Jim Bagley told his story.

"I aint got much to tell, boys," he said. "My father kept a cigar store on Eighth Avenue, and my mother and sister and I lived behind the shop. We got along pretty well, till father got run over by a street-car, and pretty soon after he died. We kept the store along a little while, but we couldn't make it go and pay the rent; so we sold out to a man who paid half down, and promised to pay the rest in a year. But before the year was up he shut up the shop, and went off, and we never got the rest of the money. The money we did get did not last long. Mother got some sewin' to do, but she couldn't earn much. I took to sellin' papers; but after a while I went into the match business, which pays pretty good. I pay mother five dollars a week, and sometimes more; so she gets along well."

"I don't see how you make so much money, Jim," said Phil Cranmer. "I've tried it, and I didn't get nothin' much out of it."

"Jim knows how," said one of the boys. "He's got enterprise."

"I go off into the country a good deal," said Jim. "There's plenty of match boys in the city. Sometimes I hire another boy to come along and help me. If he's smart I make money that way too. Last time I went out I didn't make so much."

"How was that, Jim?"

"I went up to Albany on the boat. I was doin' pretty well up there, when all to once they took me up for sellin' without a license; so I had to pay ten dollars afore they'd let me off."

"Did you have the money to pay, Jim?"

"Yes, but it cleaned me out, so I didn't have but two dollars left. But I travelled off into the country towns, and got it back in a week or two. I'm glad they didn't get hold of Bill."

"Who was Bill?"

"The feller that sold for me. I couldn't have paid his fine too. That's about all I have to tell." [2]

"Captain Jinks!" called out one of the boys; "your turn next."

Attention was directed to a tall, overgrown boy of sixteen, or possibly seventeen, to whom for some unknown reason the name of the famous Captain Jinks had been given.

"That aint my name," he said.

"Oh, bother your name! Go ahead."

"I aint got nothing to say."

"Go ahead and say it."

The captain was rather taciturn, but was finally induced to tell his story.

"My father and mother are dead," he said. "I used to live with my sister and her husband. He would get drunk off the money I brought home, and if I didn't bring home as much as he expected, he'd fling a chair at my head."

"He was a bully brother-in-law," said Jerry. "Did it hurt the chair much?"

"If you want to know bad, I'll try it on you," growled the narrator.

"Good for Captain Jinks!" exclaimed two or three of the boys.

"When did you join the Hoss Marines?" asked Jerry, with apparent interest.

"Shut up your mouth!" said the captain, who did not fancy the joke.

"Go ahead, Jinks."

"I would not stand that; so I went off, and lived at the Lodge till I got in here. That's all."

Captain Jinks relapsed into silence, and Tim McQuade was called upon. He had a pair of sparkling black eyes, that looked as if he were not averse to fun.

"Maybe you don't know," he said, "that I'm fust cousin to a Markis."

"The Markis of Cork," suggested one of the boys.

"And sometimes I expect to come in for a lot of money, if I don't miss of it."

"When you do, just treat a feller, will you?" said Jerry.

"Course I will. I was born in a big castle made of stone, and used to go round dressed in welvet, and had no end of nice things, till one day a feller that had a spite ag'in the Markis carried me off, and brought me to America, where I had to go to work and earn my own livin'."

"Why don't you write the Markis, and get him to send for you?" asked Jerry.

---

[2] The main incidents of Jim Bagley's story are true, having been communicated to the writer by Jim himself, a wide-awake boy of fifteen, who appeared to possess decided business ability and energy. The name only is fictitious.

"'Cause he can't read, you spalpeen! What 'ud be the use of writin' to him?"

"Maybe it's the fault of your writin', Tim."

"Maybe it is," said Tim. "When the Markis dies I'm going back, an' I'll invite you all to come an' pass a week at Castle McQuade."

"Bully for you, Tim! Now, Dutchey, tell us your story."

Dutchey was a boy of ten, with a full face and rotund figure, whose English, as he had been but two years in the country, was highly flavored with his native dialect.

"I cannot English sprechen," he said.

"Never mind, Dutchey. Do as well as you can."

"It is mine story you want? He is not very long, but I will tell him so goot as I can. Mine vater was a shoemaker, what makes boots. He come from Sharmany, on der Rhein, mit my moder, and five childer. He take a little shop, and make some money, till one day a house fall on his head mit a brick, an he die. Then I go out into der street, and black boots so much as I get him to do, and the money what I get I carry home to mine moder. I cannot much English sprechen, or I could tell mine story more goot."

"Bully for you, Dutchey! You're a trump."

"What is one trump?" asked the boy, with a puzzled expression.

"It is a good feller."

This explanation seemed to reconcile Dutchey to being called a trump, and he lay back on the bed with an expression of satisfaction.

"Now, Ben, tell us your story."

It was Ben, the luggage boy, who was addressed. The question embarrassed him, for he preferred to keep his story secret. He hoped ere long to leave his present haunts and associates, and he did not care to give the latter a clue by which they might trace him in his new character and position. Yet he had no good reason to assign for silence. He was considering what sort of a story he could manufacture, that would pass muster, when he was relieved from further consideration by an unexpected occurrence.

It appears that a boy had applied for admission to the rendezvous; but, on account of his unpopular character, had been refused. This naturally incensed him, and he determined to betray the boys to the policeman on the beat. The sight that greeted Ben, as he looked towards the entrance, was the face of the policeman, peering into the apartment. He uttered a half exclamation, which attracted the general attention. Instantly all was excitement.

"The copp! the copp!" passed from mouth to mouth.

The officer saw that the odds were against him, and he must summon help. He went up the ladder, therefore, and went in search of assistance. The boys scrambled up after him. Some were caught, and ultimately sentenced to the Island, on a charge of stealing the articles which were found; but others escaped. Among these was Ben, who was lucky enough to glide off in the darkness. He took the little German boy under his protection, and managed to get him safely away also. In this case the ends of justice were not interfered with, as neither of the two had been guilty of dishonesty, or anything else rendering them amenable to the law.

"Well, Dutchey, we're safe," said Ben, when they had got some blocks away from the wharf. "How do you feel?"

"I lose mine breath," said the little boy, panting with the effort he had made.

"That's better than losin' your liberty," said Ben. "You'll get your breath back again. Now we must look about and see where we can sleep. I wonder if Jim Bagley's took."

Just then a boy came running up.

"Why, it's Ben and Dutchey," he said.

"Jerry, is it you? I'm glad you're safe."

"The copp got a grip of me, but I left my jacket in his hands. He can carry that to the station-house if he wants to."

Jerry's appearance corresponded to his statement, his jacket being gone, leaving a dilapidated vest and ragged shirt alone to protect the upper part of his body. He shivered with the cold, for it was now November.

"Here, Jerry," said Ben, "just take my vest an' put over yours. I'll button up my coat."

"If I was as fat as Dutchey, I wouldn't mind the cold," said Jerry.

The three boys finally found an old wagon, in which all three huddled up together, by this means keeping warmer than they otherwise could. Being turned out of their beds into the street might have been considered a hardship by boys differently reared, but it was not enough to disturb the philosophy of our young vagrants.

CHAPTER XXIV

BEN TRANSFORMED

Ben worked away steadily at his double occupation, saving money as well as he could; but he met with no more profitable adventures. His earnings were gradual. Some weeks he laid by as much as a dollar and a half, or even two dollars, but other weeks he barely reached a dollar. So the end of March came before he was able to carry out the object which he had in view.

One morning about this time Ben carefully counted up his deposits, and found they amounted to fifty dollars and thirty-seven cents. It was a joyful moment, which he had long looked forward to. He had been tempted to rest satisfied with forty when he had reached that sum, but he resisted the temptation.

"I aint goin' to do things by halves," he said to himself. "I can't do it for less'n fifty dollars. I must wait awhile."

But the moment had arrived when he could accomplish his purpose. As Ben looked down at his ragged attire, which was in a considerably worse condition then when he was first presented to the reader, he felt that it was high time he got a new suit.

The first thing to be done was to get his money. He made his way to the savings-bank, and presented himself at the counter.

"I want all of my money," he said.

"I hope you're not going to spend it all," said the bank officer, who by this time had come to feel acquainted with Ben, from his frequent calls to make deposits.

"I'm goin' to buy some new clothes," said Ben. "Don't I look as if I needed some?"

"Yes, you are rather out at elbows, I must admit. But new clothes won't cost all the money you have in the bank."

"I'm goin' home to my friends," said Ben, "after I've got dressed decently."

"That's a good resolution, my boy; I hope you'll stick to it."

"It's what I've been workin' for, for a long time," said Ben.

He filled out the order for the money, and it was delivered to him.

The next thing was to buy a new suit of clothes. Usually Ben had procured his outfit in Chatham Street, but he soared higher now. He made his way to a large ready-made clothing warehouse on Broadway, and entered. The main apartment was spacious, the counters were heaped with articles of dress, and numerous clerks were ready to wait upon customers.

"Well, what's wanted?" asked one, glancing superciliously at the ragged boy entering.

"Have you got any clothes that will fit me?" asked Ben.

"I guess you've lost your way, Johnny, haven't you?"

"What makes you think so?" asked Ben.

"This isn't Chatham Street."

"Thank you for the information," said Ben. "I thought it was when I saw you here."

There was a laugh, at the clerk's expense, among those who heard the retort.

"What are you here for, anyway?" demanded the clerk, with an air of insulted majesty.

"To buy some clothes," said Ben; "but you needn't show 'em to me. I'll go to somebody else."

"Have you got any money?"

"You'll know soon enough."

He went to another part of the store, and applied to a salesman whose appearance he liked better. After some hesitation, Ben made choice of a suit of substantial warm cloth, a dark mixed sack-coat, vest of the same material, and a pair of pants of neat pattern.

"I won't trouble you to send 'em," said Ben, "as my house is closed for the season."

The bundle was made up, and handed to him. The price of the entire suit was twenty dollars, which was a good price for those days. Ben took the bundle under his arm and went out.

His purchases were not yet all made. He went next to a furnishing store, and bought three shirts, three pairs of stockings, some collars, and a necktie, finishing up with a pair of gloves. These cost him eight dollars. A neat felt hat and a pair of shoes, which he procured elsewhere, completed his outfit. On counting up, Ben found that he had expended thirty-six dollars, leaving in his hands a balance of fourteen dollars and thirty-seven cents.

Before putting on his new purchases, Ben felt that he must go through a process of purification. He went, therefore, to a barber's basement shop, with which baths were connected, and, going down the steps, said to the barber's assistant, who happened to be alone at the time, "I want a warm bath."

"Pay in advance," said the young man, surveying the ragged figure before him with some hesitation.

"All right," said Ben. "How much is it?"

"Twenty-five cents."

"Here it is," said Ben, producing the exact amount from his vest-pocket.

Such ragged customers were not usual; but there seemed to be no good excuse for refusing Ben, as he had the money to pay. In five minutes the bath was declared to be ready, and Ben, entering the small room assigned to him, joyfully divested himself of the ragged garments which he was never again to put on, and got into the tub. It probably will not excite surprise when I say that Ben stood in need of a bath. His street life had not been particularly favorable to cleanliness, nor had he been provided with such facilities for attending to his toilet as are usual in well-regulated families. However, he was quite aware of his deficiencies in this way, and spared neither pains nor soap to remedy them. It was a work of time; but finally he felt satisfied with the result of his efforts, and, after drying himself, proceeded to put on his new clothes. They proved to fit excellently. Indeed, they wrought such a change in our hero's appearance that he could hardly believe in his own identity when he stood before the glass, and saw reflected the form of a well-dressed boy, in place of the ragged figure which he saw on entering. The only thing which marred his good appearance was his hair, which had grown to undue length. He determined to have it cut before he left the barber's shop.

He tied up the clothes he had taken off in the paper which had contained his new suit, and, opening the door, went out into the main room with the bundle under his arm.

Meanwhile the proprietor of the shop had returned.

"Who is taking a bath?" he asked of his assistant.

"A ragged street boy," said the latter.

"What did you let him in for?"

"He paid in advance."

"I don't care about such customers any way," said the barber. "Remember next time."

"All right."

At this moment Ben made his appearance; but that appearance was so much altered that the young man looked at him in astonishment. He looked thoroughly well dressed, and might have passed readily for the scion of a wealthy family.

"Were two bath-rooms occupied?" asked the proprietor.

"No."

"I thought you said—"

"I was never so surprised in my life," said the assistant. "Did you get changed in the bath?" he asked of Ben.

"Yes," said Ben.

"What made you wear such a ragged suit?"

"I was in disguise," said Ben; "but I've got tired of it, and thrown it off. I think I'll have my hair cut."

"Take a seat," said the proprietor. "I'll cut your hair myself. How will you have it cut?"

"I want to be in the fashion," said Ben. "Make it look as well as you can."

He took his seat, and the task commenced. The barber was skilful in his art, and he saw at once what style would become Ben best. He exerted himself to the utmost, and when at the end of half an hour he withdrew the cloth from around our hero's neck, he had effected a change almost marvellous in Ben's appearance.

I have already said that Ben was naturally good-looking. But even good looks need fair play, and rags and neglect are apt to obscure the gifts of nature. So Ben had never looked his best till now. But when his hair was cut and arranged, and he looked in the mirror to observe the effect, he was himself surprised. It was some like the change that transformed Cinderella into a princess.

"I shan't be ashamed to tell my cousin who I am now," he said.

CHAPTER XXV

BEN MAKES HIMSELF KNOWN

Ben went out into the street with two bundles under his arm. One contained the ragged clothes which he had just taken off. The other, which was much smaller, contained his extra shirts and stockings. The first he did not care to keep. He therefore lost no time in throwing it into an alley-way.

"It'll be a lucky chap that finds it," thought Ben.

He next put on his gloves, and considered what he should do next. It was half-past twelve o'clock already, for he had not been able to get his money from the bank till ten, and the purchases and bath, as well as the hair-cutting, had taken up considerable time. He began to feel hungry, and appetite suggested that he should first of all go to a restaurant and get some dinner.

On the way thither he met two of his street acquaintances, who passed him without the slightest mark of recognition. This pleased Ben, for it assured him that the change which he had effected in his appearance was a considerable one.

While eating dinner, he deliberated what he should do. It was Saturday, and it would be almost too late to start for his Pennsylvania home. He decided to go to his sister's house on Madison Avenue, and make himself known there first of all. He was influenced to this partly by the desire he had to meet his cousin, who, as he knew, was making his home, while attending school, at the house of Mr. Abercrombie. He had more than once been up to that part of the city in the hope of catching a glimpse of the cousin for whom he retained his old, boyish love; but he had always shrunk, even when seeing him, from attracting his observation. He did not wish to be remembered in his rags, and so denied himself the pleasure for which he yearned. But now he was satisfied with his appearance. He felt that he was as well dressed as Charles himself, and would do no discredit to him if they were seen in the street together.

He got on board an omnibus, and took his seat. A lady soon after entered, and sat down beside him She drew out some money from her purse, and, passing it to Ben, said, "Will you have the kindness to pass up my fare, sir?"

"Certainly," said Ben, politely.

It was a small incident, but he felt, from the young lady's manner of addressing him, that she looked upon him as her equal socially, and this afforded him not a little pleasure. He wondered how he could have been content to drift about the streets so long, clothed in rags. New hopes and a new ambition had been awakened within him, and he felt that a new life lay before him, much better worth living than the old life.

These thoughts occupied him as he rode up Broadway.

At length he left the omnibus, and took the shortest route to his sister's house. When he ascended the steps, and rang the bell, he felt rather a queer sensation come over him. He remembered very well the last time he had ascended those same steps, carrying his cousin's valise. His heart beat quick with excitement, in the midst of which the door was opened by the servant.

He had already decided to ask for his cousin, preferring to make himself known to him first.

"Is Charles Marston in?" he inquired.

"Yes, sir," said the servant. "Won't you come in?"

She threw open the door of the parlor, and Ben, entering, seated himself in an arm-chair, holding his hat in his hand.

"I wonder if she'd asked me in here if I'd come in my rags?" he asked himself, with a smile.

The servant went upstairs, where she found Charles in his own room, writing a French exercise.

"Master Charles," she said, "one of your school-mates is in the parlor. He wants to see you."

"All right. I'll go right down."

The mistake was quite a natural one, as boys who attended the same private school frequently called for Charles.

Charles went downstairs, and entered the parlor. Ben rose as he entered.

"How are you, Charlie?" said Ben, rising, and offering his hand.

Charles looked in his face with a puzzled expression. It was not one of his school-mates, as he had supposed; but it must be some one that knew him intimately, or he would not have addressed him so familiarly.

"I ought to know you," he said, apologetically; "but I can't think who it is."

"Don't you remember your Cousin Ben, Charlie?" asked our hero.

"Ben!" exclaimed Charles, in the greatest astonishment. He

looked eagerly in our hero's face for a moment, then impulsively
threw his arms around Ben's neck, and kissed him.

"I am so glad to see you, Ben," he said. "Where have you been all
the time?"

"Then you didn't forget me, Charlie?" said Ben, returning the
embrace.

"No, Ben. I've thought of you many and many a time. We used to
be such good friends, you know. We will be again,—will we not?"

"I hope so, Charlie. That was one of my reasons for coming back."

"How did you know I was here?"

"I will tell you some time, Charlie; but not now. Is my sister at
home?"

"Yes. I will call her. She will be very much surprised. We all
thought you—"

"Dead, I suppose."

"Yes; but I always hoped you would come back again."

"Don't tell Mary who it is. See if she recognizes me."

Summoned by Charles, Mrs. Abercrombie came down to the parlor. She was merely told that a gentleman desired to see her.

When she entered the parlor, Ben rose from his seat.

She looked at him for a moment, and her face lighted up.

"It's Ben," she said. "O Ben, how could you stay away so long?"

"What, do you remember me, Mary?" asked our hero, in surprise.

"Yes. I knew you by your resemblance to Charles. We always remarked it when you were young boys together."

As the two boys were standing side by side, the resemblance of
which she spoke was quite striking. Ben was the larger of the two;
but their features were similar, as well as the color of the hair and
eyes, and the similarity of their dress completed the illusion. Mrs.
Abercrombie surveyed her brother with satisfaction. She had been
afraid he would be coarse and vulgar after so many years of neglect, if he should ever return; but here he was, to all appearance,
a young gentleman of whom she need not feel ashamed.

"Ben must share my room, Cousin Mary," said Charles. "We've
got so much to say to each other."

"I didn't know I was to stay," said Ben, smiling.

"You mustn't leave us again, Ben," said his sister. "Monday you
must start for home. Poor mother has mourned for you so long.
She will be overjoyed to see you again."

When Mr. Abercrombie came home, his new brother-in-law was
introduced to him. He received Ben cordially, and in a way to
make him feel at home. In the course of the morning Mr. Sampson

called, and Ben was introduced to him.

"There's something in your brother's voice that sounds familiar," he said to Mrs. Abercrombie. "I think I must have met him before."

"He has not been with us for some years," said Mrs. Abercrombie, who did not care to reveal that Ben was a returned prodigal.

"Probably I am deceived," said Mr. Sampson.

Ben, however, knew that Mr. Sampson had good cause to remember him. He was afraid the servant who had brought him his breakfast some months before in the basement might remember him; but there was no danger of that. She never dreamed of associating the young gentleman, her mistress's brother, with the ragged and dirty boy who had brought the valise for Master Charles.

CHAPTER XXVI

THE PRODIGAL'S RETURN

On Sunday evening, Ben, in company with his sister, her husband, and Charles, attended a sacred concert in Steinway Hall. As he stepped within the vestibule, he saw two street boys outside, whom he knew well. Their attire was very similar to that which he had himself worn until the day before. They looked at Ben, but never thought of identifying him with the baggage-smasher with whom they had often bunked together.

"See what it is," thought Ben, "to be well dressed and have fashionable friends."

As he sat in a reserved seat but a little distance from the platform, surrounded by well-dressed people, he was sometimes tempted to doubt whether he was the same boy who a few days before was wandering about the streets, a friendless outcast. The change was so complete and wonderful that he seemed to himself a new boy. But he enjoyed the change. It seemed a good deal pleasanter resting in the luxurious bedchamber, which he shared with Charles at his sister's house, than the chance accommodations to which he had been accustomed.

On Monday he started for Philadelphia, on his journey home.

We will precede him.

Mrs. Brandon sat in an arm-chair before the fire, knitting. She was not old, but care and sorrow had threaded her dark hair with silver, and on her brow there were traces of a sorrow patiently borne, but none the less deeply felt. She had never recovered from the loss of her son. Her daughter Mary had inherited something of her father's self-contained, undemonstrative manner; but Ben had been impulsive and affectionate, and had always been very near his mother's heart. To feel that he had passed from her sight was a great sorrow; but it was a greater still not to know where he was. He might be suffering pain or privation; he might have fallen into bad and vicious habits for aught she knew. It would have been a relief, though a sad one, to know that he was dead. But nothing whatever had been heard of him since the letter of which the reader is already aware.

Since Mary's marriage Mrs. Brandon had been very much alone. Her husband was so taciturn and reserved that he was not much company for her; so she was left very much to her own thoughts, and these dwelt often upon Ben, though six years had elapsed since he left home.

"If I could see him once more," she often said to herself, "I could die in peace."

So Mrs. Brandon was busily thinking of Ben on that Monday afternoon, as she sat knitting before the fire; little thinking that God had heard her prayer, and that the son whom she so longed to see was close at hand. He was even then coming up the graveled walk that led to the house.

It may be imagined that Ben's heart beat with unwonted excitement, as the scenes of his early boyhood once more appeared before him. A thousand boyish memories returned to him, as he trod the familiar street. He met persons whom he knew, but they showed no recognition of him. Six years had wrought too great a change in him.

He rang the bell.

The summons was answered by the servant, the only one employed in Mrs. Brandon's modest establishment.

"Is Mrs. Brandon at home?" asked Ben.

"Yes," answered the girl. "Will you walk in?"

Ben stepped into the entry, and the girl opened the door of the room in which Mrs. Brandon was seated.

Mrs. Brandon looked up.

She saw standing at the door a well-grown lad of sixteen, with a face browned by long exposure to the sun and air. It was six years since she had seen Ben; but in spite of the changes which time may have wrought, a mother's heart is not easily deceived. A wild hope sprang up in her heart. She tried to rise from her chair, but her excite was so great that her limbs refused their office.

"Mother!" exclaimed Ben, and, hurrying forward he threw his arms around his mother's neck.

"God be thanked!" she exclaimed, with heartfelt gratitude. "I have missed you so much, Ben."

Ben's heart reproached him as he saw the traces of sorrow upon his mother's face, and felt that he had been the cause.

"Forgive me, mother!" he said.

"It is all forgotten now. I am so happy!" she answered, her eyes filled with joyful tears.

They sat down together, and Ben began to tell his story. In the midst of it his father entered. He stopped short when he saw Ben sitting beside his mother.

"It is Ben come back," said his mother, joyfully.

Mr. Brandon did not fall on his son's neck and kiss him. That was not his way. He held out his hand, and said, "Benjamin, I am very glad to see you."

In the evening they talked together over the new plans which Ben's return suggested.

"You must stay with us, Ben," said his mother. "I cannot part with you now."

"I am getting old, Benjamin," said his father. "I need help in my business. You must stay and help me, and by and by you shall have the whole charge of it."

"I am afraid I don't know enough," said Ben. "I haven't studied any since I left home. I don't know as much as I did when I was ten."

"You shall study at home for a year," said his father. "The teacher of the academy shall give you private lessons. You can learn a great deal in a year if you set about it."

To this arrangement Ben acceded. He is now studying at home, and his abilities being excellent, and his ambition excited, is making remarkable progress. Next year he will assist his father. Mr. Brandon seems to have changed greatly. He is no longer stern and hard, but gentle and forbearing, and is evidently proud of Ben, who would run a chance of being spoiled by over-indulgence, if his hard discipline as a street boy had not given him a manliness and self-reliance above his years. He is gradually laying aside the injurious habits which he acquired in his street life, and I confidently hope for him a worthy and useful manhood.

From time to time Ben visits New York, and renews his intimacy with his Cousin Charles, who returns his warm affection. Charles, in turn, spends the summer at Cedarville, where they are inseparable.

So we bid farewell to Ben, the Luggage Boy, hoping that he may be able to repay his mother in part for the sorrow which his long absence occasioned her, and that she may live long to enjoy his society. To my young readers, who have received my stories of street life with so much indulgence, I bid a brief farewell, hoping to present them ere long the sixth volume of the Ragged Dick Series, under the title of

Rufus And Rose;
Or,
The Fortunes of Rough and Ready.